To Kill a King

To Kill a King

By
Madeleine Polland

HILLSIDE EDUCATION

Cover and interior book design by Mary Jo Loboda

Cover art by Sean Fitzpatrick

ISBN: 978-1-7331383-8-3

Hillside Education
475 Bidwell Hill Road
Lake Ariel, PA 18436
www.hillsideeducation.com

CONTENTS

Chapter One

"Eleven," thought Merca. "Eleven, I was when I first came here."

She looked about her in the warm bright tower of the palace of Dunfermline almost as if she had just arrived. It was the court of King Malcolm and Queen Margaret of Scotland, living now through a time of peace with the Norman king who had conquered England in 1066, more than ten years past. For a long time, Malcolm had refused to submit to him, and they had known bitter war, but now he was come to an uneasy peace with England, offering reluctant homage to Norman William as his overlord.

Merca had been dreaming much of late; thinking backward and forward through her life, as though at sixteen she had reached some age where she must stop and recollect herself before she could go further. As though going on was somehow difficult, and she must understand herself before she faced it.

It was not that she was unhappy about her future. Whenever these vague anxieties overtook her, she rushed to tell herself that her life would be exactly as she herself had chosen. Exactly. Exactly. In her years in Dunfermline she had grown into a worshiping reflection of Queen Margaret herself. But she, Merca, would go further than the queen.

Margaret had dedicated all her life to the service of God and His poor. "Feed the hungry," He had said on earth, and the queen had charged herself to this task through all her kingdom of Scotia. But—and here Merca shook her head in faint, bewildered disapproval—the queen still allowed herself the distractions of her home and family; her love for the huge, red-bearded Malcolm; her devotion to all things beautiful; her passionate pleas that God would find no special good in ugliness.

All this Merca was determined to leave behind, although if anyone should ask her why, she could only look at them in something close to fear and offer no reason; only this fierce need to turn her back on all that was soft and kind and beautiful—on the world that was Dunfermline. As soon as the snows broke from the northern glens, she was to leave for the hospice founded by Queen Margaret at Kilrymont, to give shelter to the thousands of exhausted pilgrims flocking there to venerate the relics of St. Andrew. The queen had seen their need and bidden a house of holy sisters set up a place of rest and shelter.

A house of holy sisters. The candlelight in the warm room seemed to Merca to fade away. The cries of the children and the soft laughter of Queen Margaret came as from another world—as though she had already left them and found the solitude and silence she was determined on. Prayer and silence, and nothing to think of save God and his pathetic poor. Her eyes grew wide and dark with some self-centered pathos as she thought of the paths by which God had led her to His service, her mind swerving aside as memory took her too far. Abruptly she stood up.

"Madam," she said to the queen, who sat at her embroidery frame, two of her small sons beside her arguing about the colors in her design. "Madam, please have I permission to go and meet my brother?"

The queen glanced at the shuttered window, closed already against the bitter dusk.

"So late?" she said. "So cold?" And was surprised by a look almost of panic on Merca's face. "Very well," she went on at once. The child must want to see Dag very much.

Merca did not want particularly to see Dag. That was merely an excuse. Every evening she could manage it, she went to the church on the slope of the hill below the tower. Always she drove herself to go at dusk, when the great mass of the unfinished church was full of threatening gloom, barely touched by the small stars of tapers on the distant altar. It was like leaving Dunfermline. It was something that she had to do. Surely God would think her prayers better that she should offer them from her conquered fear; or her unconquered terror that held her wordless and rigid every evening in the dark. She did not understand herself; but she must do it; must do everything that was cold and dark and ugly; must turn from beauty and happiness and peace; from comfort and even from love itself. From love above all. From Queen Margaret and from Dag. From those who made life itself for her. She did not understand, tears of sheer confusion often secret on her face. She did not understand, but she must do it.

Only when she felt sure of where her future lay— in silence, piety and loneliness—did she grow calm; bemused to some feeling of happiness and safety. Of course she would be happy. Like Dag. She would be happy in Kilrymont as her young brother was happy here. From the first day he had arrived in Dunfermline, he had been drawn to the black-robed monks who had followed Queen Margaret to Scotia and settled in the wattle monastery down the hill. Dag was concerned with no splendid call to leave the world as she was. He was drawn instead by some vague important happiness growing from tall tapers crowned with misty gold about a distant altar; peace and strange excitement from men's voices singing sad, flat, shapeless music which belonged to God alone; quiet ordering of days where everyone was always doing something but no one was ever in a hurry. Above all he knew the wild, secret pleasure of finding that his fingers knew how to hold a brush and pen without being told; following the placing of color and fine gold as the monks had taught him, turning plain parchment into a field of blazing beauty; knew quickly how to shape the letters which they told him would leave the Word of God for other boys to read long after he was old and dead.

"What is it, sister? You look to me as if you have the colic." She had not expected to see him, but Dag was always unexpected, waiting for her here above the wild, snow-drifted glen as if he knew that she was coming. Maddening, infuriating Dag, who was half of her own heart, who always said the wrong thing to her, and said nothing of himself. Yet who seemed to have some secret of content that she had never touched.

"I am cold," she said shortly, and would tell him nothing of her feelings. Although he would never laugh, he would look at her with blue, considering eyes and make some foolish comment to drive her into a blaze of temper. Then there would have to be hours of saying penance for her anger in the cold chapel, that she could so betray the serene and spiritual image of the queen she tried to copy. She was cold too, fresh come into the biting frost from beside the warm logs.

"I am cold," she said again. "What are you doing here at this time of day?"

He did not answer her, his mind full of the enchantments he had left.

"Do you know what I did today, sister?" he said then. He smiled, but his eyes looked inward, as though he was smiling at himself. "I did a letter, on my own, in the missal Brother Andrew is composing."

"No!" cried Merca, suitably impressed, for this was privilege indeed. At the same time, she wondered why it was that Dag, who was certain to become a monk, never talked of God, or all the holy thoughts and prayers that should surely occupy his day; and that she tried so hard to think of all the time.

"Something else," he went on. "Just for fun, I copied my shell in among the flowers which frame the letter. It was a P. Just for fun."

His shell! Not for years had she thought of it. A shell that was his talisman when he was small and frightened, until he had felt safe and happy, and given it to the queen. His shell.

"Just for fun!" she cried then, horrified. "But Dag, my young brother, you do not put things in holy books for fun!"

Dag shrugged his square shoulders in the black cape and his mild eyes gleamed.

"Why not? Why not?" Suddenly he looked bored. "I'm cold too," he said. "I'm off to the kitchens to get some job where it's warm."

Merca looked at him and thought of the great hearth in the monastery kitchen with the fire red below the simmering pots. There they cooked for all Queen Margaret's poor as well as for the monks. She hunched her scarlet cloak around her and for one moment looked back up at the shuttered windows of the tower room she had left. Above the dark tangle of the snow-patched glen the sky was grim and heavy with the promise of more snow to come, candlelight already gleaming warm in the dwellings on the slope below, the courtyard empty in the bleak twilight. She turned to follow Dag.

"I will walk down with you," she said. "I am going to the chapel."

Sideways, Dag looked at her and did not answer. He noticed only that lately she seemed to have grown much taller. Now he had to look up to talk to her. Not that she had much to talk about, except being holy.

The minster was newly consecrated to the Holy Trinity, a dream in pale unweathered stone of the piety and holiness of the queen who built it. Below the curved doorway with the chiseling of its chevrons still fresh from the tool, Merca paused and looked at Dag.

"Are you not coming in?"

Dag swiveled around appalled blue eyes.

"What, I?" he cried. "To say more prayers than they shall make me? Not I, dear sister."

The girl looked at him, baffled, knowing he mocked her. Never could she reach his feelings, except they were about some piece of lettering or the colors of some flower he picked to wave beneath her nose about the summer glen. "Not I," he said again, and drifted on down the hill, square and enigmatic, leaving her only the faint suggestion of his bland smile. Merca turned and pushed through the wattle screen that waited on the door, thrusting down her shaking fear.

"What need have I of Dag," she told herself desperately.

"Am I not in God's house and will He not care for me?"

But she knew that this was not enough.

"Pig," she said then, into the empty church, and forgot about the penance for being angry. "Pig," she repeated. "To refuse to come in when I am afraid!"

Anger cheered her and helped to calm her fears. Still furious with Dag, she dropped on her knees determinedly, for the prayers that privately even Queen Margaret thought too many.

In the warmth and comfort of her tower chamber, the queen's fingers threaded delicately in and out the splendid colors of an altar cloth for her minster. The fair head bent above the frame was little faded from the bright gold that had held Malcolm's eyes when he first met her in London, in the spring. Her gentle face was beautiful as ever despite the two small sturdy boys tumbling in the rushes with the dogs, the baby in his wooden cradle, and Ethelred who sat quietly on a stool beside his mother. Edward, her eldest son, was with the men somewhere in his father's absence; in the tiltyard or the stables or the forge.

She lifted her head and looked across the fire at Mary, her waiting woman, close to her as long as she had been in Scotia.

"We must think to get ready for the feast of Yule," the queen said, and Mary looked at her with pity, knowing her thought that King Malcolm would be still away.

"And Prince Edward's birthday," she said quickly to cheer her, and saw the queen smile.

At a fierce yell from the floor, she bent down and removed the bone which Edmund had found among the rushes and was trying to push in Edgar's eye. Throwing it into the fire, she turned to distract Edgar's yelling with a few strands of bright silk, which he stared at wide-eyed, the tears upon his face.

"Merca is long gone," the queen said then, as if the scrambling of the babies showed some lack of care.

Mary did not look up. "She will be in the church," she said tartly.

"I know," Queen Margaret said, and her patience echoed none of Mary's irritation. "Foolish child! Who has taught her such nonsense? Not I. God wants her love and happiness, not her fear."

Mary shrugged. She had cared for Merca since she was a child, but lately her strong, practical nature had been irritated by the girl's preoccupation with her soul.

"You know Merca," she said. "You know Merca, Madam. She was always thus. Nothing for her is by the half-measure and, at the moment, she has no use for this plain world of ours. All is for God."

Absently, the queen laid down her needle. "But Mary, she is not happy."

Mary shrugged again, but the queen's eyes were distant.

"Why?" she said, almost to herself. "Why is she so unhappy that she flees the world? Have we perhaps not made her happy?"

"Well," she said then, easily, "soon she will go to Kilrymont and learn to know her heart."

When Merca came slipping back out of the bitter dusk, the air about her cold, the queen was kneeling at the fire, her babies around her with their small, inexpert palms together, round knees restless in the rushes, saying their evening prayers before their supper.

"Pater noster," she said for them carefully, "qui es in coeli." After her they said it as best they could, knowing nothing of the words they said; only the sweet security of the firelight and their kneeling mother, her voice saying these words each evening as though she loved them. When she was long dead, and they were kings and princes of the church in all their state and power, the familiar words of the "Pater Noster" would still bring them strength and peace.

Merca slipped to her knees beside the children, trying to keep her mind on her prayers, and not give herself over to the delicious agony of the fire reaching out to thaw her fingers. The queen, she felt sure, would never know such weakness.

Even as she argued with herself, the queen blessed herself and stood up.

"I have mind for nothing at this time," she said. "Not even my prayers. I hope God will be gentle with me." She sighed. "It is the first time my lord has raised his sword in years, and I had hoped it was hung up for good."

"But dear Madam," said Mary. "He had to go. The men of Moray were risen in rebellion. Your royal husband would not stay much longer king if he sat at home beside your hearth and let every upstart run his kingdom wild."

The queen smiled at her risen flush and angry eyes. "He would be well to have you fight beside him, Mary."

The woman blushed and looked abashed, but her eyes did not soften.

"Your pardon, Madam." She dropped a quick curtsy, and told herself to watch her tongue. Next she would blurt out that there were those, such as her own brother Dougal, who thought that Queen Margaret made her husband Malcolm softer than became a king; who thought you could not run a kingdom with nothing else but love; who would have been glad to have back the old Malcolm whose only language was the sword and who used violence for diplomacy.

Beside them, Merca gathered up the hands of the two small princes to hold them from fresh mischief until the summons came to supper, but her gesture was absent, her mind filling with this creeping fear that always filled her when people spoke of war; as if she must turn at once and run and run, she knew not where.

There would be no war in Kilrymont. No war. No love. Nothing. Peace and God and nothing more.

Through the sharp cold air came the slow winding of the horn, summoning all the palace to its supper. The smile faded from Queen Margaret's face. It was at this time she missed her husband most, when the horn would bring him, with small Edward on his shoulders, from falcon run or armory or tiltyard, the night frost clinging to their clothes, their two faces alight with interest in the things that only a man could teach his son. Their two faces so alike; their two smiles first only for her.

Edward burst in through the curtain of the door, and for a moment she could hardly look at him—so small and square and so like the huge Malcolm, it was as if God had made a jest.

Carefully he bowed to his mother, and then came and leaned against her, the king's son, a small, tired boy like any other. Merca, watching them, already troubled and disturbed by talk of war, knew suddenly a wave of desperate grief. For what, Mother of God, for what, she asked, and did not understand herself. Grief, and with it the same fear of war and battle and darkness; fear for what and grief for what she did not know. She herself had chosen her life in Kilrymont. She herself was determined on her future. Why then this stab of blind unhappy fear, this sense of dreadful loss that was in some way familiar, as if she had known it all before. Barely could she look at the firelight and the warm rich room, and the red-gold head of the lovely queen bent tenderly above her little son. Queen Margaret kissed Edward and took his hand. "Where have you been?"

"In the forge. Arthur has been teaching me to beat out a spear."

"Then my small smith is hungry."

Grave and self-important, but with big eyes flickering eagerly over the food, Edward sat beside the queen on the high seat, in the absence of his father. On the walls hooks were empty save for the triumphant shields and spears and axes of warriors long dead in glory. Along the laden tables, the queen had bidden the household come up close together. The women, the very old and the very young, the few house carls left to guard her and her children in their strong tower; it was the shrunken household of a king gone off to war.

Graciously, she smiled at them as if they were her valued guests, and reached to take the first meat from the platter.

"Come, little ones," she said. "Now you may begin.

"It is not for me," Merca told herself coldly, fear and confusion crushed back. "It is not for me."

She reached for a small dry piece of bread and a sparse bone, turning then to the children who were her duty.

Chapter Two

Yule was long past and the first pale colors of spring flaunting the bitter sunsets, before Malcolm came riding home from Moray, hard ahead of his men. It was as though in the instant that he turned his face to home and Margaret, he shed some harder brutal self, the harsh Viking warrior with blood his business and the sword his life, sliding incomprehensibly into the Gaelic dreamer who had hung his weapons on the wall and learned the peace that she alone could teach him. The thought of her fair face beckoned him like a lamp, urging his tired horse southward through the melting slush and overburdened rivers, thrusting from his mind the ravaged country and the burned-out homesteads he had left behind. When he was away from her he knew the need to fight; knew the need to stay for weeks in this rebellious district until every upstart spark had been suppressed. There would be no more rebellion in the kingdom, now that news would get abroad of his revenge on Moray.

Yet now that he would turn again to Margaret and to

home, he felt faint shame creeping that he must tell her how the thing had gone. As though he could have found some other way. He hunched his head against dark driving rain, and his long mouth tightened. These things he must know for himself, and it was over now.

He crested the long slope of the moors, and even in the darkness and the bitter cold, there was some wild sweetness in the air, telling of the abandoned winter and the spring to come, when they would go back to their small strong fort above the green waters of the Firth of Forth. Below him lay the lights of Dunfermline, and for one moment he slowed his great black horse to look at them.

The queen was in the middle of a game of blind-man's buff with all the little boys.

"Edgar's turn," she said, and the small round-faced boy bounced before Merca.

"Edgar," he shouted. "Edgar. Edgar's turn."

"Be still then," cried Merca, "or I cannot tie the blindfold," but the two-year-old could not be still until his mother took his hands.

Malcolm came in unannounced through the curtain of the door, word of his coming flying through the dark fort outside. It was then Margaret herself who wore the blind, groping with gentle helplessness among her small screaming sons. Tiny though they were, they knew their father for the king, and on the instant stopped their shouting and their scrambling, leaving the queen alone and groping in the middle of the floor, stricken herself with sudden stillness, her hands growing quiet on the cold wet wool of Malcolm's cloak as he moved into her path. With an abrupt gesture, Merca moved to gather the little boys, turning her head deliberately from the look upon their faces.

Not even to Dag, to whom she could tell everything, although she got little help from his mild listening face, could she tell of this strange unhappy disturbance that shook her when she watched her king and queen together among their children.

"They are not like other people," was all she could say to him lamely the next day, telling of Malcolm's return, and the spurning of all the feasting that should greet a returning king. It was simply a quiet supper in the queen's chamber, crowded by excited little boys, Edward leaning speechless with content against his father's arm.

"They are a king and queen," Dag said practically. They moved about the tables in the great refectory beside the monastery that was given over to the daily feeding of the poor, laying out the bread and meat handed to them by a round-faced brother through the serving hatch. Merca clucked impatiently.

"That is not what I mean," she said. "Dag, you are stupid."

Dag raised his thick fair brows and continued to lay his pieces of bread so that they made a pattern on the middle of the table; pleasing colors too—the rough brown bread against the pale scrubbed timber.

"I am as God made me," he said amiably, and Merca glanced at him sharply. She never knew when Dag was laughing at her.

"I mean—" she blundered on, and the breadbasket was laid idle on the table. "I mean they are not like other people who are married," and again Dag's quizzical eyebrows rose and he gave her no help.

"Were it not," said Merca earnestly, "that I know the queen, my lady Margaret, to be the holiest in all Scotia, indeed of Christendom, I might sometimes think she loves King Malcolm more than she loves God." Her thin intense face was filled with the enormity of what she said, eyes wide with unwilling disapproval. Now Dag turned on her one long blue gaze.

"It seems to me, sister," he said flatly, "you think a little much of God, and talk of nothing else. Let God talk to you instead."

Merca stared at him. It was always thus. Dag said so little, always letting her chatter on to his impassive face, and then when he spoke he said something that gave her no help at all, and often she did not understand.

"God talk to me?" she said amazed. "And who am I that God should talk to me?" Secretly she was embarrassed, that Dag somehow might have penetrated the most secret dream of her mind, when she saw herself raised to such heights of perfection in the life she had chosen that the world might remember her saintliness forever. Saint Merca! How could Dag know? He couldn't, for if he did he would laugh. No one must laugh. Only by being certain of her own future in God could she hold her senseless fears at bay. At the very thought, her cheeks flamed scarlet, but Dag was not looking at her, staring instead out of the open door, away toward the long slope of the hills where the snow broke into patches on their dark sides.

"Yes," he said then, and did not turn. He could not express himself, but he thought Merca talked too endlessly of God, as though He could be found only in this nuns' place she was going to. His long lower lip came out. He did not want her to go away and shut herself up with these sisters where he might never see her more. He frowned, fair heavy brows drawing down, and then he sighed. He was only ten, and he did not want his sister to go away.

He turned back toward the tables before the brother in the hatch should have time to scold, and Merca knew she would get no more from him. She went on with her task, careful and orderly, a thin tall girl who moved now with instinctive gentle grace in all her gestures, her narrow face beneath dark drifting hair too tense for beauty; only her rare sudden smiles telling of another Merca. There was something about her that held the other young people around the royal court at bay.

Dag watched her as she walked away from him down the long chilly room, and with a careful gentle smile and gracious inclination of her head, bent to take another basket of bread from the old monk. Dag growled. She was being the queen again. Why couldn't Merca just be herself? It was good enough for him.

On the windy spur below the tower, Malcolm came up from the stables to join his wife where she walked among her ladies in the bright unstable sun. Seeing him come, they fell back and let the king and queen walk alone, on to the lip of the glen where the ground fell steep below the wall to the tumbling river at its foot—favorite playground of the small tempestuous princes.

"Look, Malcolm!" cried the queen. "Look! The snow is still on the hills, but here the alders have a sheen of yellow. Spring is not far away!"

Malcolm grunted. Always she saw beauty wherever she might walk, binding his rough spirit, although his mind could never follow her. Spring to him meant no more than yet another journey, and now he must bring himself to tell her so. He took the edge of her flying cloak and pulled it round her against the wind, as though he would protect her even when he was gone.

"Then we shall go back, my love, to Edinburgh?" he said. If he must leave her, then there she would be safer—safer against the threat of war that was her own most dreadful fear.

"If you insist," she said, and smiled at him. "You know my heart is in Dunfermline." Here they had been married, and here started their life together in the crude wattle hutments that had then been the royal house of Scotia.

"Sweet Margaret, I do insist," he answered her, and could not look at her, "for I must leave you once again. No, no," he cried in answer to her cry and the sudden whitening of her face, blue eyes wide with fright and horror. "There is no trouble! No war! I must go on business about my English manors. It is tedious but necessary.

"I must go myself, and in some small state, for I must see the king."

Margaret made a small face and in the instant grew as young as her own children.

"To think, Malcolm," she said, "that most of their lives, King William lives in London, and his lady over in Normandy. It would not do for me!"

Malcolm took her hands, frank delight on his face that his exquisite queen should love him so, crude monster that he was. He kissed the small hand vanishing into his strong paw.

"Nor I, sweet," he said. "Nor I."

Merca saw them as she came up the hill from the refectory to the tower, and turned away her scarlet face, flooded with her usual embarrassment that her king and queen should seem like ordinary people with the same love which had once torn her for the little helpless Dag. She halted, startled by her own thought.

"But I still love Dag," she thought, desperately. Still loved Dag, but no longer knew how she should show it, when she no longer needed to look after him. Blindly she groped after some thought that she could only care about people if she might serve them and look after them. As she would serve the poor, she comforted herself firmly, in God's name. And love them. Disturbed, she brushed aside the thought of Dag, who needed so much to love her, and went on swiftly up the hill.

Beside the king, Queen Margaret stirred with a small gesture of despair, looking after the awkward young back.

"What is it?" Malcolm asked her.

"No problem of my lord's," she said. "No problem of my lord's."

"Come," said Malcolm. "Come with me down to the stables, and choose the harness I shall wear for riding into London."

"Oh, Malcolm." Behind her, her ladies moved to follow—accepting with complete affection that wherever her royal husband led, she would follow, and they must follow too, despite the cold wind and their soft shoes. The queen too had but a light cloak and little shoes of scarlet cloth.

"Oh, Malcolm," she said again.

"Yes?"

"Almost I would come with you."

Malcolm's big bearded face was ablaze with eagerness.

"And why not? Why not?" Sadly she shook her head.

"Too many children, and too young. When they are grown, we shall ride the world together. But London. Malcolm, you know that by the time you are there, the flowers will be out along the river."

He stopped and looked at her, a moment of perfect

tenderness in the cold Scottish wind above the glen, as they remembered the long-gone day when they had met, beside the stream in Westminster, where Edward the Confessor, last of the Saxon kings, was building his great church. Long ago, in a London spring.

"I will go there for you," he said, and suddenly the queen's face lit with pleasure.

"I will send someone for myself," she said, and shook her head to his questioning look. "You said you go in some state?" she asked him, and he nodded.

"Well then," she said, picking her way around the puddles on the low slope of the hill. "Well then, it will do you no harm to take some ladies."

"Ladies!" Malcolm was horrified. On these regular journeys of homage to William, he had used to hunt and drink his way down England. "I want no care with ladies!"

"Malcolm!" She was firm. "I have long promised Mary that on one of these journeys she should go to see her sister who lives in London. Long promised.

"You take their brother Dougal every time, but Mary never goes and she grows lonely for her sister. This time, Dougal and some other gentlemen can care for the ladies, so it will not hamper your hunting and your drinking. Though I doubt," she added, "the arrangement will suit Dougal very well."

Malcolm grinned. How well she knew him, his love; so gentle in herself, yet never would she deny him his own rougher pleasures.

"Well," he said truculently, unwilling to give in too easily.

"They will only want your escort," she said, and knew his objections done. "And with Mary and Dougal," she was thinking to herself, "I shall send the little Merca, to let her see the world beyond these walls, before the convent takes her."

Merca forgot all her manners, staring at the queen in wild astonishment when she told her of the plan.

"I, Madam?" she said, and could say no more. Her face echoed none of the excitement flooding Mary's with high sudden color, her brown eyes full of happy tears. Merca looked from her to the queen in dawning distress.

"I, Madam? But what would I do in London? It is so far away."

How could she tell them of the blind, terrifying panic tearing her at the very thought of venturing out again, even under the escort of the king and all his carls, into the wider world where once she had almost starved to death. It was just to be managed in the springtime, when the queen would have taken her to the sisters of Kilrymont, safe forever beyond the reach of the world in any way. She did not want to go to London, or indeed to anywhere! Black fear took her. Like an animal trapped, she stared desperately around the warm chamber, hung with bright colors, floored with rush and fur.

"No, Madam—I beg you—I do not want to go to London! Let me go at once to Kilrymont if you do not want me here!"

Queen Margaret was startled by her distress; she had thought the girl would be pleased to have the chance. Beside her, Mary clucked her tongue, halted in her own delight. Trust this one never to be ordinary. But the queen moved gently to the girl who had turned pale as the candles unlit on the chest, and stood shaking on the edge of tears. She put her arm around her, and looked close into her face, trying to fathom the secret miseries she did not understand.

"Merca, Merca, child, of course we want you here. But I watch you and am not sure myself that it is right for you to go so soon to Kilrymont and leave the world."

"It is what I want, Madam," protested Merca. "What else is there for me?" she added, and did not know why she said it. As long as she could remember she had wanted nothing but to be like the queen, and to give her life to God and His holy work, without even the earthly tie of marriage. The queen caught eagerly at her last words.

"What else is there for you?" she asked. "There is all your life for Kilrymont. For now, you can go to care for Mary, and see the great minster built by our last Saxon king near where I met my lord; see London and the wide river where the ships come from all the world; maybe see the palace of the Norman king himself." She paused and smiled, fair face soft with tenderness. "See London in the spring," she said, "when the kingcup flowers are out along the Thames. Mary shall care for you."

Mary looked as though she would gladly let her stay at home.

"Why her majesty must coax her to go, I cannot say," she said later to her brother Dougal. "We have no need to be burdened with her when she would rather stay at home."

Dougal was not much concerned. He would not ride with the king, as he had done before, Malcolm relaxed and easy, away from all the cares of kingship; the ale good and the deer fat in the green English forests. This time he was saddled with a pack of women, and what of one more or less? He shrugged.

"The queen knows best," he said, and with that Mary had to be content, forgetting Merca in a sudden panic of her own about her shifts and petticoats and kirtles, none of them good enough for London, where she might see the Norman king.

"London?" said Dag, and even he looked solemn and

impressed.

London was a place that took a long time to reach and must be very far away. "Many of our fathers in the monastery have been to London."

"And what do they say of it?" asked Merca fearfully, and Dag blinked, trying to remember.

"They talk only of the great minster," he said at last, and knew it was not much help.

"It is the journey," Merca whispered then to Dag, as though she could not say it, but somehow was compelled. "It is the journey." And Dag looked at her, and remembered nothing he could put into words, but knew her fears, their eyes locked in recollections of journeyings they could never manage to forget. Dag recovered first.

"This time," he said practically, acknowledging all they had not said, "you will be with the king, and the king's men. You can come to no harm."

Reluctantly Merca nodded.

"Still I would rather go straight to Kilrymont." Then she drew herself up and composed her face into the dutiful expression that always irritated Dag. "But if my lady the queen says I must go to London, then it is my duty and I must go."

Dag looked at her sourly.

"Have a care, my sister," he said. "Have a care lest you enjoy it."

Chapter Three

L ong before the cavalcade rode off toward the south, Merca had tried the patience of the ladies with her cold indifference to their excitement.

"Look!" cried Mary to her one evening, her dark eyes bright with pleasure and triumph. "I have lined my old red cloak with fur, see, and retrimmed the sleeves, and it will do me most excellently for the journey."

Merca looked up from her needlework.

"What journey?" she asked. "Oh, to London. Yes," she added with bored politeness, looking at the cloak as if it were some offense against her God. "It will do well indeed."

Mary's quick temper flared at last; she had held her tongue too long.

"Well, I know what madam my lady thinks, but for myself, Mistress Merca, I would rather that you stayed at home when you care so little for the journey! We do not want your whining voice!"

She was contrite the moment she had spoken, turning from Merca's shattered face to make a quick curtsy of apology to the queen, who only sighed.

"Do not distress yourself, Mary. Merca, it is true you try us all, when so many of us would gladly take your place. Think you that I do not want to go to London with my lord?"

Tears of anguish rose in Merca's eyes that she should have offended her beloved queen.

The queen lifted her head from the length of dark red velvet which she stitched for Merca, picturing it with pleasure against the long dark fall of the girl's hair.

"Do you think she is old enough to know better?" she asked Mary, and her eyes grew dark and sad. "Who knows, Mary? This I tell my lord, that the dreadful tracks of war are left across a land to mark it through the time of generations. Who knows then how long they may leave their mark on people?"

Wide-eyed, tears arrested, Merca stared at her, and then with an abrupt sob, ran without permission from the room. The queen stared after her with pity.

"No, Mary," she said. "Merca is not old. Sixteen years she may be, but her mind for some reason is closed to the world in which she should grow up, and so she stays a child, full of a child's dreams."

They had to summon all their patience to be calm with her.

"Why, Madam?" she asked the queen when she was called in with all the excited ladies to a bower piled with silks and wools and velvets from the queen's stores. There were fine heavy wools from Scottish sheep to keep them warm in the cold early days of spring, bright silks brought half across the world, and velvets out of France. "Why, Madam, what need have I for clothes?" Merca said.

The other ladies clucked with irritation and astonishment, but the queen said patiently: "Dear Merca, you are going into a wider world than our small Scottish Court. Will you have them think we are all savages up here, and do not know how to dress?"

Merca looked on coldly. It was not for her. It was this rich beauty-loving side of her adored Queen Margaret from which she would flee. Above the piles of pretty fabrics, the soft heaps of fur and trembling fronds of feathers, her young face was hostile.

"For other people, Madam, maybe that is true. But for me, who goes into the cloister the moment I am back? What need have I for such as these? A plain black robe or two will do for me."

The queen looked at her thin pale face set in disapproval of such frivolity. Why must this stiff-necked child make everyone dislike her so? Where had she herself failed her that she could only give such narrow love, and never know to love the world itself and all the gifts of the God she talked so much about? Clothes she must have.

Merca's bony wrists were growing out of the worn sleeves of her black gown, and her ankles showed underneath its hem. Yet for all her awkwardness, she had a strange and delicate beauty, reminding the queen more than once of the small white windflowers that blew in the glen before winter was even past. Now, even in her cold detachment, her beauty had some quality that told the queen she was not in truth a nun. God did not want mistakes. She must try and coax and warm this frail chill winter flower. Her smile on Merca's face warmed and deepened.

She took her hand, aware that her ladies thought her foolish to take so much trouble.

"Merca, child, can you tell me who has taught you ever that God cares not for beauty? I cannot think this true. If He did not, He could not have made this world. He could never have made as much as one sunset. I am sure your small brother Dag knows this already."

Merca looked at her sharply, ready as always to be wounded by the smallest hint that she had fallen short of the standards of her beloved queen. Pricked too by bitter sudden jealousy that Dag should be set as an example to her. Dag who did not care, but did exactly as he pleased, while she strove all the time to be so good, and only for Queen Margaret's sake.

"Dag?" she said.

"Yes, dear child. Dag, of course. He knows that even one strand of silk in all its lovely color, or one sunset, is a gift of pleasure from God and we must treasure it."

"But Madam, God did not make the silk."

"No," the queen was still patient. "No, but He gave men skill to make it in His name. And," she added with a smile, "gave us ladies skill to wear it, and delight in it in His name too."

Merca did not understand. If you would serve God, then surely it were best to leave the world and all its pleasures, and think of nothing else. She was almost on the edge of tears, feeling the hostility of the other women; struggling in her own confused mind to do what she had decided to be right. She realized the queen was smiling at her, closely, gently.

"Will you dress to please me," Queen Margaret asked, "and to hold up my name in London, in pride?"

Through her haze of puzzled tears, Merca nodded, and the queen reached for the length of ruby velvet she was already fashioning, crying out loud in pleasure at the way it immediately warmed the girl's tense, chilly face.

"Child," she cried, "you will be beautiful!" At once she knew she had done wrong. Under the glowing folds across her shoulders, Merca grew taut, and the tears cleared at once from cold, disinterested eyes. She would not even look at it.

"I will wear anything," she said, "that my lady queen commands."

Quietly the queen removed the velvet and let her go.

"She looked so sad," Merca said later on to Dag. "Suddenly she looked so sad." Now she was fretting again that she had displeased the queen. "Why should it matter that I am given to God, and do not want fine clothes?"

"Beautiful," the queen had said. She did not want to be beautiful.

Dag shook his head, his eyes on a piece of soft clay he worked between his fingers. A moment ago it had looked quite like a bird, but now something had gone wrong.

"It may be Madam the Queen thinks," he said abstractedly, "as I do, sister, that you are touched in the head to refuse. I wish I might have a tunic of ruby velvet." He ran a slow, thoughtful finger down his black tunic of coarse wool, as though he felt under it the soft satisfying pile of velvet. "I would not refuse, that must spend my days all of my life now in this crow's habit."

She looked at him in astonishment. "But you want to!" she cried.

"Oh, yes," Dag said, agreeably. "I want to. But a little while of ruby velvet would be good."

Merca stared at him, recalling what the queen had said.

"Would you think it belonged to God?" she asked him desperately.

Dag turned big blue eyes on her. "What?"

"The tunic. The tunic of ruby velvet!"

Dag gave one of his rare, deep laughs. "I would be sure, sister, that it belonged to me and no one else."

Merca gave up, more than ever confused; knowing only that despite all they said, she had no wish for beauty; compelled by this feeling of confusion and fear toward the sisters in their prayer and isolation at Kilrymont; toward the shearing off of her long, lovely hair and the gray shapeless, woolen robe.

It was what, she told herself firmly, Madam the Queen would have done if she had not met King Malcolm.

"Look, sister," cried Dag. "Look, I have made myself an eagle!"

Queen Margaret stood to watch them go, when at last the day came, her small boys jumping round her skirts, and the baby in her arms for a last look at his father. Malcolm drew rein beside her on his great black horse, wolfhounds skirmishing about its hooves, and the small Edward before his father in the saddle, clinging to its mane with excited fists. Malcolm slid him gently to the ground, and quelled the clamor of the others with a glance, turning to look into his wife's face.

"Sweet Margaret!" he cried. "Enough! I am not going to war. Remember I am allowed to go wherever I may wish, as long as I go not to war!"

She laughed then, acknowledging the jest they made of her deepest and most dreadful fears. "Mercy of God," cried Malcolm, "I must go. This is no place for me!"

The Queen laughed outright then, seeing his appalled and rueful face as the ladies of the party clattered out of the court behind him. She let him go reluctantly, for God knew, however peaceful his intentions, it was not difficult for Malcolm to run into trouble. But he'd be hard put to go a-fighting with this lot at his heels.

He was already gone, in a sudden clatter of hooves and arms, his men behind him, leaving a decent space between him and his embarrassing flock.

Merca rode behind Mary's brother Dougal, attached to the court, like her, since Malcolm and Margaret had first settled in Dunfermline. Dag lifted a silent hand to her, a smear of ink across its fingers. Would he see her again, he thought suddenly, before she went into this closed place at Kilrymont, and he might never see her more. Desolation took him. Merca. Sister. He stood tearless, but as though suddenly he could not see well, and then the queen's hand reached out for his, and she drew him into the circle of the little boys.

"Come, Dag," she said, "and be with us today. For without the king we shall be lonely and in need of you."

Dag's face cleared to careful manners, and he bowed to the queen above their clasped hands.

"I will show Your Majesty and the small princes," he said deliberately, and she could not bear to look at his lonely, formal face, "how I have taught myself to make an eagle."

Merca had been too occupied to give much thought to leaving him, busy with her own cold resentment that she must go at all. Dag was all right. Dag was always all right, because he was allowed to do what he wanted. She would be happy too, if she were not forced to go out into a world she did not want. But suddenly the sight of his round fair face, standing out wide-eyed and silent from the cheerful crowd, struck her with the real knowledge of their parting. As though she read his mind, she too was gripped with sudden grief, piercing her cold selfish misery.

"Dag," she whispered. "Dag," but no one heard her, lost in the gay farewells of an excited journey. Her few painful tears left dark unhappy patches on the back of Dougal's velvet coat, and then her pale face came up again, and Dag was gone, hidden by the turn of the spring-flooded road. London and all the world before her.

Two days later they were riding through Northumbria.

"And it were well," Mary sat with stricken face, "that Madam our Queen is not here to see all this."

No one answered her, all the company silent with grief and horror at the weed-grown ravaged countryside through which they had ridden since the early day. Land that had all the looks of being once fair and cultivated, ramped with brambles and wild sapling trees, nettles standing man-high in abandoned gardens and pushing through the doors and windows of roofless cottages and burned-out fragments that must have once been barns and byres. Here and there along the road through the green wilderness, from some fragment of a habitation, a wretch or two would creep, more often than not maimed with the deadly professional maimings of an angry conqueror; whining and begging for food they had almost forgotten how to eat.

From Malcolm and his men that followed him, they would flee in terror. To them an army had one meaning only, but they clung and clamored round the bright cavalcade which followed until the ladies wept with horror for the starvation and disfigurement; the fearful ugliness that seemed beyond the hope of even God to help.

Wider and wider grew Merca's watching eyes, staring

round her almost unaware of those that whined, starving at her horse's stirrup. The green abandoned countryside, overgrown to shapelessness, nagged her like a half-remembered dream; something she should know from a long past time she had forgotten. Her mind stirred and shivered on the-edge of grief she could not reach.

"Who?" she breathed to Dougal, when they passed a group of dilapidated hutments struggling to grow once more into the bright prosperous farmstead it had once been. "Who did it? Malcom, our king?"

Dougal looked right around at her in shock.

"Malcolm!" he said. "This is what the Normans did on their way into Scotia, when they would have destroyed the whole kingdom had not Malcolm and the Conqueror's brother Robert made for wiser councils, and come to the treaty they have held since."

The Normans. Merca remembered. She had been with Queen Margaret then, and they had all gone to Dunkeld for safety. Edward was a baby. When they came back they found Dunfermline burnt to ash. That was the Normans. But surely she knew more of them. Something earlier.

"The Conqueror," she said then, and Dougal nodded, glad to talk of anything.

"The Conqueror," he said then. "He is overlord now by treaty to our own King Malcolm. That is why we make these journeys. Every so often Malcolm must come and do homage to the English king. He has agreed on it. So he keeps his kingdom."

And hangs up his sword, thought Merca, which is what my queen wants.

"You may see him," Dougal went on in his deep soft voice, which she could feel rumbling through his back. "A great fierce man With eyes like marble, and a heart as cold. He does not brook any to defy him."

Merca did not speak again, her eyes wandering silently over the ruined country, under the cool bright sky.

It was not yet dusk when they approached the shabby remnants of a village of some size. Most of it had been patched and rebuilt with battered timbers, new thatch bright and yellow on the roofs. There was an inn, with a great oak spreading out above it, half its thatch new-laid and half as old and weathered as the oak itself.

There was a nervous landlord with no ears and no fingers on his right hand, who shook with terror at the sight of the arms and soldiers but did not dare refuse them lodging lest once more his thatch go flaming to the skies above his head. He looked amazed when a little later the ladies clattered into his torch-lit court.

"Madam, I am not fit for ladies," he protested to Mary, and Merca could not take her eyes from the poor red holes where once his ears had been. The Conqueror. With cold eyes and colder heart. "My inn, Madam, my inn is not what once it was." His stump of a hand gestured at the weeds and brambles growing almost to the door. "It is but lately I have come back at all."

"We will not ask much, landlord," said Mary gently, and the man blinked as though kindness was something he had long forgotten. "Just a chamber where we may rest the night, and some water to refresh ourselves.

Mary smiled at him then, her warm friendly smile, and hesitantly the man smiled back, hobbling off in his coarse tunic and ill-made boots to do her bidding.

The sun was setting in wild trails of pink and rose behind a small round hill fringed with trees, soft and black against the evening sky as the feathers of the bird who fluted of the spring in the old oak above the roof. Somehow Merca could not follow the other ladies inside, tired and thirsty though she was after the long day's journey. Irresolute, she stood a moment in the yard, silent amid the bustle of the settling of the horses.

Then, almost as if she were walking in a dream, she moved out through the gate. The soft muddy road led down a gentle slope to where the forest closed on both sides; but to the left along the forest edge there was a path, much overgrown, but beaten in the spring growth as though it had been lately used again.

Silent she stood, and in the falling evening the forest was a black wall beyond her; behind her the black twilight sky and the jingle of harness from the small inn where lights pricked out in sudden welcome, as they must have done before the Conqueror's wars, and the destruction—when Northumbria was fair farming land of prosperous people, tilling their crops and caring for their children. Merca moved a blind uncomprehending step toward the path into the woods, and her mind groped for words she had not used in five long years.

She remembered nothing, but, "Mother," she whispered, and "Father."

Suddenly she began to shiver. "Dag!" she cried aloud. "Dag! Dag!" Then she began to run, fleeing back up the muddy road to the small lights and the safety of the inn.

But Dag was not there either. Only Mary, just beginning to get alarmed that she was missing, hustling her to her evening meal without a glance.

Chapter Four

The barren and ravaged country of the north was like a remembered nightmare as they came down into the springtime softness of the northern midlands.

"Though, York, they tell me, is a heap of cinders still, and men stripped of all they own have no heart to rebuild it."

"Chester, too, he razed to the ground, that it dared to stand against him."

Merca listened to the conversation passing back and forth and thought this Conqueror from Normandy must surely be a monster. No wonder the queen would not have King Malcolm fight against him!

"But why, Mary?" she asked in the end, for it did not seem sense to be sacking and burning the cities of his own kingdom.

She looked round her where they had stopped for rest beside a small river babbling clear beneath a little wooden bridge. Round yellow flowers twined with bright blue along its edges, fat cattle browsed beyond it in a pasture growing to their knees.

"And the kingdom is so fair," she added reluctantly. This was the world of beauty, and she wanted none of it, wherever she might find it.

"Because," answered Mary, surprised and pleased that Merca should think of anything outside herself at all. "Because even to this day, this Norman William holds England only by the sword—by killing any who would rise against him and destroying all their lands."

Merca fell silent, bending to splash her face in the clear stream, where small disturbed fishes flashed like quicksilver above the stones. She paused a moment and watched them. Dag would like them. They would make him smile, so small and quick they were, and so foolish that they did not seem to know which way they were going. But she did not smile herself, her hands falling limp into the water, for the thought of Dag, for some strange reason brought back like a cloud of darkness the thought of the path beside the forest.

"It was but a dream," she told herself firmly, and bent to dip her hands again, among the flashing fish. "It was but a dream."

Determinedly she turned her back even on the memory, as she would close the door against everything on this journey. Only her return would be real, when she could leave this world that was proving even more full of fear and ugliness than she had thought while she was secure these last years in the shelter and affection of the queen.

By the time they reached the flat land from which they could see the great Abbey of Saint Alban, reared upon its Roman hill, the ladies and their small protecting cavalcade were on their own. King Malcolm and his followers had ridden off into the dark rolling forests, following the hunting that alone consoled him for these long journeys of homage to William.

Merca watched them go.

"We will be safe?" she asked Dougal. Only odd words of some anxiety ever broke her cool, disinterested silence.

"Of course." He laughed. "There are enough of us yet," he said. "But," he added, "for all they say of Norman William, it is true enough that he has made England safe with laws. They say a man can ride from one end to the other with his bosom full of gold, and take no harm."

Merca was surprised into speech.

"I would not wish," she said vehemently, "to walk a step alone in that poor country to the north, which he has ravaged."

"It's nice round here," he said hopefully. Maybe at last she was about to talk. Dougal was tired of the silence. It was a long journey, and many times he'd wished his sister had given him some cheerful chatty wench to ride pillion with him, instead of this cold young beauty.

Merca looked away at the green fields running into the woods, clean-carved along their edges like a piece of wood; the yellow catkins dancing on the hedges; the pads of pale primroses carpeting the mossy banks, and the sweet fragrance of the hidden violets when the sun broke through the windy clouds. It was the world and she did not like it.

She was happier when they visited the shrine of the martyred Saint Alban, and with cold stone beneath her knees she could forget the world in prayer as she had not done since she left home. Reluctantly she followed them when she was bidden, and they threaded round the city until they came to the old Roman road; straight as a knife blade through to

London, thronged with pilgrims plodding to and from the shrine.

In a cool evening full of birdsong, colors etched with all the agonizing clarity of spring, they came to the crest of a long gentle hill, leading away down into the vast shadowed mass that was the city, pricked with the first lights of evening. Even Merca's silence held a breath of wonder.

"We shall live in that?" she asked.

Mary was already kicking her horse, unable to waste even one moment to look.

"We shall live in that," she said, "and with my sister." Delightedly she beamed at Dougal. "I have not seen her almost since I was a child. We shall be with her by curfew."

Mary's sister had married a Saxon wool merchant, whom she had met when he once journeyed north to purchase wool. He was a man of substance, serving even the Norman court, with a cool civility that told them nothing of his feelings. He dwelt in a fair wooden house of good size some distance along the river bank from the king's own palace of Westminster.

There was much hustle and clamor in getting the horses into the stables, torchlight flaring above the dark river down below the wall, and much crying aloud as to where in Mercy's name all this great force of gentlemen might sleep. Then they were dismounted and passing through great wooden gates into a quiet court with the lights of dwelling rooms warm and bright all round it; and Mary and Dougal and their sister talking ceaselessly since the moment when the sister had come running, calling, all the way into the stableyard to meet them. Mary's sister seemed to Merca's weary eyes to be but Mary once again, but older; gray hairs thick in the black about her rosy face.

"For I could not wait, dear child," she said to Mary, who smiled and smiled with tears lying on her cheeks. "I could not wait to give you formal welcome in the hall. My husband and family shall do that."

"Family?" thought Merca. She had not thought of family. Frivolous girls maybe, who would bother her from her devotions, and her determination that she would think of nothing in this strange place but her queen whom she must imitate in all ways, and her God, to whom she would give her life as soon as she went home. She shivered suddenly in the cool night air, and felt a friendly arm about her.

"And who is this?" It was the sister, Gundred.

"That is Merca," said Mary. "She is one of the queen's adopted ones, and comes now to care for me!"

Guiltily Merca started. This was what the queen had said, that she should care for Mary and for her clothes, and sew for her and look to all her needs. And on this long long journey, she had given it no thought; Mary indeed had cared for her. But what of it. She had not wished to come, and in the world she would go to as soon as she returned there would be no care for clothes or hair or things inconsequent like that.

She shared Mary's chamber, remembering her duty to please the queen sufficiently to pour Mary's water that she might wash, looking curiously at the tall earthen jug, unlike the heavy stone at home. The furniture too was lighter—frail after the carving of the north—the bed little more than a platform flung with furs and skins and soft, colored blankets in the wool that was the master's trade.

The master himself waited for them in his hall, long and light with curving beams looking as though they could scarce support the roof. He stood beside the great fire in the center of the floor, his long tunic cut in the Norman fashion, and his fair graying hair so cut also, a thick cap above his still-handsome face. Kindly he kissed Mary and bade her and Dougal welcome to his house, his wife moving restlessly about, unable to keep her eyes from Mary's face, Dougal she had seen on earlier journeys to London with his king. Merca stood and knew her worst fears true. There were two girls: Constance, much the same age as herself, and Mary, younger, who both wore their bright dresses as though they loved them, tossing their transparent veils excitedly about their long fair curls. Eagerly they kissed Mary, and giggled at Dougal's cheerful teasing. At last they were settled down beside the fire, and "Ah," cried Gundred. "I did forget the little one."

Unwillingly, Merca was drawn forward, to meet the two girls who greeted her with candid pleasure, warm happy smiles on their open Saxon faces.

"No trace, you see, Mary," cried their mother, as though she read Merca's very thoughts. "No trace of my dark hair and all my blood from Scotia. Three Saxons have I borne, and not one single Scot!"

She looked with glowing pride at her two fair girls.

"But where three?" said Mary. "Where is Edward?"

It was as though the smallest fraction of a shadow fell, as the tiniest cloud will dim the sun for one second on a flawless day. Then the mother laughed and shrugged.

"Edward is seventeen," she said. "And who knows when a boy of seventeen will come and go."

Merca listened with disinterest. No boy of seventeen would be concern of hers.

It was difficult to remember that she was not interested in the world when she was taken to walk about the town of London. Night and day the thunder of wooden wheels filled the narrow streets of beaten earth, rumbling along with the trade of half the world. Edwin the wool merchant was kind, and glad to tell Mary all he knew about his city, pointing over his walls to the tall ships rocking downstream in the deep river, their cargoes packed in wagons to go to every corner of the kingdom.

Everywhere were rising the strong defensive buildings of the Conqueror. In the palace itself, the maze of wooden buildings was giving way to stone brought specially from Caen in Normandy, that William's walls might give him a sense of home in this land that hated him. Away down toward the sea, beyond the misty haze of masts that filled the moorings of the port, four square towers were rising— the new fortress of London. Up the river, beyond the palace rose the twin spires of the new minster of the Confessor, its dedication his dying act.

"And may I go to the minster?" Merca asked, her mind full of all Queen Margaret had told her. "May I go to say my prayers?"

Mary and Gundred looked at her, and on Mary's face was familiar irritation.

"Would you not rather go with us to see the markets and the streets of London—there is a man brings a dancing bear each day outside the palace, hoping that the king may call him in."

The two fair girls laughed and clapped their hands.

"Oh, yes, he is so droll. And Merca," cried Constance the elder, "there is a ship new in from the east, my father tells me, and the cloth merchants will have all its cargo! New from the east!"

She had never seen a dancing bear. She had never seen a bear. Silks she had seen in plenty and they were all the same! Obstinately she shook her head into the silence falling round her.

"I would go to the minster and say my prayers."

That first day Gundred insisted on a waiting woman going with her. They had all accepted with bored and civil faces that she was a prig, as Mary had warned them. Merca put her nose into the air and told herself fiercely that she did not mind. She had but little to offer God if her resolution wavered the moment she got into this crowded humming city that, for all her determination, touched her with some secret excitement she had never felt before. Firmly she kept her eyes down, and walked along the walls, watching only the skirts of the woman in front of her to lead the way.

She could not resist a glance at the high stone walls that grew about the palace, the huge wooden gates guarded by tall odd-looking soldiers, with long tunics and the nose pieces of their helmets covering almost to their mouths. She shivered suddenly, as at some threat she had forgotten. The soldiers at Malcolm's court she had learned to take for granted, with their broad swords and swinging saffron kilts, and bare legs red and hardened with the cold. There was some greater menace in these tall clean men, with warm good clothes and gleaming spears. Quickly she hurried after the woman, who turned around to wait for her.

A causeway had been built out across the marshes to the minster, and Merca sought in vain for the small winding path where Queen Margaret had met Malcolm. But beyond the causeway along the river edge, the kingcups grew as bright and yellow as they had done for Margaret, and in the gentle sun, Merca stopped suddenly and smiled, her rare sweet sudden smile that so changed her guarded face.

The woman was waiting again, clearly impatient, twitching at her blue cloak, and clucking irritably.

She was equally impatient when Merca at last came out, a little bewildered because even in the cool incense-laden shadows of the minster, she had not found the peace she sought. She was still conscious—even between the pious hands locked before her face—of the city lying beyond the causeway, as though life itself worried at her from within its walls.

It was the woman, she told herself. It was not possible to pray with her waiting there outside, counting all the time that Merca was gone. The second day, she faced bravely to Gundred, before the disgusted Mary and the girls who were going to take a boat and a hamper of food, and row themselves up into the country along the springtime river.

"I know the way, now," she said. "I would rather go alone."

Gundred shrugged. Impossible this child, and she had best be left to do exactly as she wished. It was not far to the minster, and the city was safe, that was one thing this monster William had done. Between the hours of curfew, the youngest could walk safely abroad and come to no harm.

Merca could hear their laughter floating across the water as she let herself out of the small side door of the house. Suddenly she wondered what it would be like to go too; to laugh and jest as these two girls, and see the soft southern country for herself. She thrust the thought aside. Her promise was to God, and she would not want to break it just because the kingcups were out along the river in this disturbing city.

"I wish," she heard Constance calling, "I wish Edward were here."

She had forgotten Edward, nor did she think of him now.

She found more peace in the minster, listening to the toneless singing of the black-robed monks who performed their noon office. It made her think of Dag, and a stab of deadly loneliness shot through her for his round calm face. Dag. The hot tears she could not help seeped through her fingers. What was she doing here so far from home with these gay, worldly girls. All she longed for was the safety of Queen Margaret's voice, or the cool nothingness of the nunnery at Kilrymont, where she could push away this world, clamoring here so loud she could not even pray.

Behind her she heard the great door scream back upon its hinges. The last monks in the procession leaving the high altar looked behind them, and the scattered people at their prayers turned as though they had been summoned. Before she could collect herself, Merca's tear-stained face turned round with all the rest.

It was a boy, standing in a shaft of sunlight pouring from the high windows of the nave, panting as if he could go no further, each whistling breath filling the corners of the silent church. His thick fair hair was standing ruffled, as though he was new come from a flight, and his brown tunic torn off down one shoulder. Almost furtively the praying people looked toward the monks, and then one by one gathered up their bags and bundles and scuttled feverishly for the door, edging around the boy with sidelong glances as though they begged him not to see that they were there. In a few moments, the last monks vanished also, and only Merca stayed. Still kneeling she turned toward the boy, who breathed more easily now, but never moved, his eyes watching stolidly each poor frightened citizen who crept past him, lifting then to watch the monks vanish from the high altar. At last he came slowly round to look at Merca, with cool eyes full of calm consideration, widening a little as they absorbed the pale beautiful face, still clearly marked with tears.

"You are not afraid?" he asked her then, and still did not move.

She blinked, as though one of the carven saints around the walls had spoken. "Afraid?" she stammered. "Of you?"

Why should she be afraid of him, this tall thin boy with the sun on his rumpled hair? Afraid of swords and soldiers and starvation and even death. These things long ago she had learned to be afraid of. And of that path in Northumbria. Slowly she looked about her, and realized she knelt alone with him in the sun-striped shadows of the empty church. Were the others all afraid of him?

"Should I fear you?" She did not know what else to say.

The boy moved a step and shook his head.

"Where do you come from that you do not know that when a man seeks sanctuary, it is not always honored by his pursuers? You need not fear me, but before God you need fear those who follow me."

She began to get up from her knees, and quick as a flash he was across to her, giving her his hand to help her. Astonished, she took it, warm and dry within her own, filling her with some strange sensation that she did not understand. The only hand she knew familiarly was Dag's small clever paw, which was always wet with ink or paint, or even mud. She struggled to clear her mind.

Sanctuary. This she had heard of, that a man pursued for crime might seek protection on the high altar of a church, and there neither law nor enemies could touch him. Instinctively she glanced at the altar. It was yet a long way off, and the door much closer.

"What have you done?" she said then. "What have you done?"

"Nothing," he answered, "that any righteous man who loves his country would not do."

She shook her head. She did not understand. "You are a criminal?"

"Not I. Call me by any name but that!"

"Then what?"

He did not answer her. The great door swung again, and in the instant that he made to bolt up the long aisle toward the altar, he stopped, turning back. Through the opening came a dark, cheerful youth, his smile obscured a little by a trickling smear of blood from a wound under the thick thatch of close-cropped curls. Like the fair boy, he was dirty and bedraggled, and his clothes awry. But as soon as he saw him, the fair one grinned also, and anxiety fell from him as though it was his tattered tunic.

"You got away!" he cried. "Manfred! You got away!" Vigorously he thumped him on the back, and Merca felt herself a lonely outsider to some splendid danger shared; some victory that was not for her.

"Mind," cried Manfred a little thickly. "Have a care. Some churl loosed my teeth. Hit too hard and I will lose them!"

"All is well?" the fair boy asked then, more urgently.

Manfred nodded, feeling his tender teeth.

"Quite well. I lost them in the alleys by the river. But we must go, lest they think of looking here."

They had not noticed the coming of the prior, softly and silently down the long aisle, his hands in his black sleeves. Suddenly he stood beside them, a dark quiet ghost.

"My brethren tell me, son," he said, "that you come seeking sanctuary." Gentle his voice and mild his face, but something said in his demeanor, that if it were so then the reason need be a good one.

Blandly, the fair boy turned to him, and for one second Merca thought of Dag, who would have been thus smooth and friendly.

"No, my lord prior. No. We thank you for the offer. I did but wish to show my friend your lovely minster."

Coolly he bowed, and Manfred bowed with him, and his blood dripped on the pale floor. Merca could see both boys shivering on the brink of helpless laughter.

"Come Edward," said Manfred then. "I have seen enough."

The fair boy turned to Merca, his eyes regretful, as though he would have spoken longer.

"Your servant," he said. The heavy hinges creaked, and he was gone.

The prior sighed and turned away, and Merca looked at the closed door, her face creased into a frown.

Edward! Gundred's son was tall and fair and Saxon. And had not been at home these last two nights.

Chapter Five

If it were Edward in the minster, then still he did not come home.

Through the lengthening days of spring, with pale light soft as doves above the river, Dougal was away now, waiting on the king and the house was given over to the women. Edwin only came in from his warehouses as the torches kindled in the evening; presiding at his table, and asking the day's doings with amiable kindness. Merca noticed that never did he speak as though he missed his son, or even question where he was. Nor did any of the others, after Mary had cried out on that first evening.

Merca knew they found her dull, and grew more quiet and withdrawn from laughter and chatter and gay expeditions in the country and along the water. Daily she went determinedly to the minster, trying to match her prayers here in distant London with the prayers she knew her beloved queen would be saying in the small chapel perched on the pinnacle of rock at Edinburgh. This way she felt safe.

She needed desperately to feel safe. And she was lonely. Sick and desperately lonely for Queen Margaret and the little boys—and for Dag, with his round face and inky fingers. Lonely, with only Constance and her sister, who were too kind and well brought up to say so, but clearly thought her a dull and pious fool, and she was too proud to tell them otherwise.

"Safe!" she said aloud one afternoon, when once again they had gone off and left her, with disinterested smiles, bright mantles blowing in the wind. Dougal and the other gentlemen were taking them to watch the rowing races on the river where big, muscled men competed for the privilege of being boatmen to the king.

"Safe," she said again, little above a whisper, and the bright glow of the fire hazed in sudden tears. She did not understand herself. She did not want to go and see these races on the river. Panic filled her at the very thought. She wanted to go, as always, to the minster and match her devotions with the queen's. Why then these tears, hot and desperate as though she longed for something she had not got? "I will go to the minster, and be safe there."

She did not know that, in her misery, she had spoken out loud, alone, she thought, in the great hall, where smoke eddied in the draughts of spring.

"And why would you be safe in the minster?" asked a voice behind her. "Seeking sanctuary, as I did?"

The boy had been watching her some while, coming quiet into his father's hall—to find her there who had filled his mind like some elusive dream for days. What was she doing here, in mercy's name? When he spoke to her she whipped round as though some hostile sword had pricked her, big dark eyes still filled with tears. Like a fawn, he thought, taken from its mother in the forest, trembling on the edge of terror, without understanding what might threaten it.

Edward was seventeen, little older than Merca was herself, but a Saxon grown in Norman London, where a boy must early learn his mind and stick to it, if he had the courage. And if he had the courage, then there was little that would keep him still a boy. His eyes on her were quiet and thoughtful like his father's, gentling the timid animal he had startled. Carefully he smiled, easily, seeing her senseless fear.

"You do remember me?" he asked her, and she nodded, breathing hard to clear the shaming tears. All her efforts to close out a distracting world could not subdue her quick intelligence, and almost at once her own confusions faded before some question here that needed answer. It had been Edward, bruised and bloodied, in the church. Did his family know? What was he about, that he should be in such a predicament, and they not speak of him, as though he were already dead? He watched her eyes sharpen, and knew his little fawn not as simple as he had supposed.

"Sanctuary? No, good sir," she said. "I did but go to pray."

"For safety?" he asked her, and she could not answer him. Carefully she gave him the same cool look she turned upon the girls, and all he did was marvel at the clear, exquisite line of bone that shaped her jaw, trembling faintly still, as she looked at him.

"My prayers concern myself," she said, and he made a small grimace. He liked her better frightened.

"And who is myself, that I find alone in my father's hall?"

Unwillingly she told him, because she could do no less, a guest within his father's house. Already she was beginning to feel uncomfortable under the frank admiring eyes, losing the quick courage roused by curiosity.

"I travel with your mother's sister, out of Scotia," she said formally.

"Ah," he said, "I heard that she was coming. In the train of Malcolm, King of Scotia, is it not?" For a long time he considered her, as if he thought of other things beyond herself.

"And why," he asked then, "are you not with my mother and my sisters, wherever they might be. Do they neglect you, that you are like this alone?"

"I am happier to go to the minster for my prayers."

He made a long mouth and drew a considering hand across his chin. In faith there was not much happiness about her, her big eyes dark again with fright. But he nodded as though it was most commonplace.

"I shall walk with you there," he said, and saw her gaze sharpen.

"You!" She spoke before she could prevent herself. "How can you, who must be a felon, go forth into the streets?"

Thick fair eyebrows rose up to his hair.

"I beg you not to call me that," he said, and she was at once embarrassed, pushed into a sense of intimacy that frightened her, yet she must challenge him, her chin lifting.

"Then why were you about to look for sanctuary?"

Life and spirit fired her face, and he smiled to see the pale miserable girl so changed. But he would not help her.

"Ah," he said. "Ah, that is something else."

She moved then toward the door, trapped by unwilling friendship, and at once he moved to keep her. When might he see her again, if things did not go well, this pale windflower who could light to rosy spirit and so change he could not take his eyes from her. His thought of her was the same as Queen

Margaret's had been, some frail perfection reminding him of the small white flowers of the winter woods, where more than once he had spent longer time than he cared.

"Tell me," he said. Anything to hold her. "Tell me, do you not enjoy this London of ours at all?"

Merca was recovering herself, pale with the effort, but determined. All the long journey, and London itself, had not managed to distract her from her set purposes. Why then should this boy?

"I did not want to come," she said. "Nor do I look at it overmuch now I am here. I tell you, sir, I am happier in my prayers."

Like Queen Margaret again, Edward looked deeper than Mary and his sisters, who would have sighed and turned away from her priggishness.

"I'll warrant you are not," he thought, "and do I but get the time, then I will prove it to you."

Still she edged toward the door.

"And have you," he went on calmly, as though she spoke to him gladly, and cared for all they talked of. "Have you yet seen our king?—our royal William, out of Normandy?"

She glanced at him sharply, at some undertone in his voice, but the fair face was smooth and expressionless. His eyes were dark, dark gray and very large, singularly intent upon her face, as if he memorized it lest he might not see it long. She moved restlessly under his gaze; but answered, compelled by some unwilling interest in this king who had done to Northumbria a violence so terrible.

"No," she said. "I have not seen him. I am told that he is not in London."

"Of course," said Edward. "I did not know when you had arrived; I thought you might have seen him before he went a-hunting. In this new forest he has made," he added, "out of the farm lands of our people, that he may take his sport. Well, let him take it. There is a curse on his forest, and they say that it will take his sons."

Merca's eyes widened a little. The dark gaze was no longer intent upon her face, but looking inward with some fierce anger; looking clearly at the Norman hunting on the land of Saxon farmers thrown to starve.

"My own king, Malcolm, I am told is with him," she said then.

"Ah, him." Edward dismissed him. "Once the Saxons thought him their hope and strength, but now William binds him in friendship. Even Hereward," he added darkly. "He binds to him. Friendship is a heavier chain than iron would ever be. He is clever, this William."

"The queen," Merca said, and heard almost a note of apology in her own voice. Edward looked at her. "It was Queen Margaret," she went on, "who begged King Malcolm not to go on fighting with the Normans—for violence, she says, will be his death and hers. That is why she fears it so. For years, for her, he has hung up his sword, and wars are not for him. He is friend to Robert of Normandy, who is this William's son, I believe, and whom the queen thinks to be a fine and gentle man, holding war as profitless as she."

He gazed at her and her earnest words went past him, his eyes widening in pleasure to see this frail, closed creature talk suddenly so much. Her cheeks warmed again to high soft color. She too had realized how much she had said, and knew it was more than she had said to anyone for months, catching her lower lip in white even teeth, and looking at him in astonishment.

"I know you know of kings," he said gently, "for you have

lived in the household of one. But what would you know of wars? These are for men alone."

He did not know what he had done; what he had said to freeze in one second the spark that had begun to kindle her to life. Her eyes dropped and before him her face grew small and tight; the stiff unhappy face of the girl he had first seen in the minster. In a moment, she was gone.

There was no comment in the family on Edward's return; unexplained as was his absence.

"Ah, my son," Gundred said quietly when she came into the hall before the evening meal and found him seated by the fire. And if for one second she hesitated, and looked at him a little closely as though she searched for something, then only Merca noticed it. Her determination to stand aside from everything in this London world was sorely tried by curiosity. Her mind nagged at the oddness that so let Edward come and go as if he had been missing merely from the morning meal. Even his young sisters ran with pleasure to kiss him welcome, but showed no surprise that he was back; nor asked where he had been or how he had fared.

Closely she watched until the tall father came, but dusk was already falling and the candles guttering along the tables. She could not see his face, only hear his greeting, as calm as all the others, bidding his son welcome home, as he took his place at the table head.

"I should have asked him myself," Merca thought, "when I was alone with him this afternoon." But then there was this thing that he had said, of her knowing nothing about war, bringing with it as such talk always did, this fear and loneliness that haunted her like a drifting ghost which would never come to rest. Please God the king would soon be done with all his business with the Norman, and she could go home; and then to Kilrymont, where there would be silence, and peace, and safety. She did not want to talk to people—especially this boy with the warm, watching eyes.

By evening she was calmer, and ready to watch them all, that she might probe this secret. But through the meal they smiled and talked and asked each other of their days, and laughed to hear how Mary had all but fallen in the river, not knowing how to wield a pair of oars.

"I shall teach you," Edward cried to her. "I am the best oarsman in the family."

Mary tilted her head on her long neck and smiled at him her thanks, and then they talked of other things but never a word of Edward's days. The joints were stripped along the board and the baskets of bread run nearly empty before Edward laid down his knife and turned idly to his father.

"And when," he said, "and when does our good Norman king ride back to London?"

Edwin did not lift his head, delicately picking the last tasty fragments of meat from a bone. He laid it down regretfully and wiped his fingers on the cloth at his side.

"I am done with that," he said. "Good meat, wife, good meat."

"The king," he said, and stopped, lifting his head as they all did every night when darkness fell, to mark the heavy penal tolling of the curfew bell—clearing the streets of every living soul from then till dawn, under pain of death or mutilation. He only went on when the last cold boom had died away, and silence fell on the darkening city. "The king," he said easily then, "comes back into London four days from now, riding from his forest up through Winchester."

No one said anything, and Merca looked from one of them

to the other with a strange impression that they would speak were they alone.

"I would see him," she said, suddenly, loud into their silence, and did not know why she said it, frightened even as she spoke the words. "I would see him, this Norman king."

She felt their faces large as the shields on Malcolm's walls, all turning toward her in surprise; fair and dark, young round eyes and older thoughtful ones, and it was Edward who answered her.

"Then I shall take you," he said, and Merca heard his father check some explanation. It seemed that only Edward was there, a little across and opposite her, the others faded into the haze of candlelight, the boy's eyes on her in surprise and pleasure.

"But you," she said to him, with all the awkwardness of one who seldom spoke; but now she must know, and did not know how to ask her questions gently. "But you. Will you be here, that you come and go as you do?"

She felt him glance at his father, and then the father answered.

"My son, child," he said, "goes about my business in the country, for how can I weave woolen cloths for you and for my girls if I have not someone first going out to buy the fleece."

His face was open and easy, and Merca felt the hot flush of shame creeping to her eyebrows. What else? Why had she not thought of it, that she made herself so much mystery. They took no heed of his goings and his comings, because they were so used to them. And she had blurted out her rough question at his father's table.

Scarlet, she mumbled her thanks to Edward, and was not helped by the open look of amusement on his face.

It was only when they had left the board, and stood about the fire in the bang and clatter of the servants moving out the trestles, that she reared her head suddenly and looked at him again. It was not necessary, surely, to seek sanctuary from being a wool merchant's son about his lawful business. But Edward sat among his family by the fire, plucking at a Norman lute and begging mercy for the discords, the girls at his feet and his mother tranquil at the frame of her embroidery. Almost, Merca felt herself the victim of some dream, telling herself firmly that she had indeed seen him, blood on his hair and clothes torn, in the Confessor's minster. For the first time since she left Scotia, she looked clear and sharp at those about her—even Mary, who made as little comment on Edward as did everybody else. And why? Had Mary not cried out in curiosity about him in the very minutes they arrived?

In the days before the coming of the king, the atmosphere in London sharpened, everybody moving just a little faster, the tall guards on the palace gates a little brisker; an air of tension and expectancy and not a little fear, that soon they would again be under the critical cold scrutiny of their king.

"I do not think, child," said Gundred to Merca on the morning of the day William was to ride into the town. "I do not think that you should go to the minster today to say your prayers. Say them here in the house, for there are great crowds abroad today, and you may not be safe alone."

The girl blinked at her, and flushed a faint embarrassed pink, bewildered that until Gundred spoke, she had not even thought of going to her prayers. Guilt took her, and distress that even a king should have been allowed so to distract her; she turned and walked out of the dwelling that she might be alone to try and think how she could have lost herself. She leaned against the wall above the quiet river, a warm corner in the sun, with the stable jutting out to shelter her, and a little way behind her, the arch opening into the yard itself.

There was small time for thought, Edward's voice catching her ear almost at once, resentful and disappointed.

"And why not, Father? Why should I not?" he asked, and she heard the father answer clearly. They must be walking in the yard just the other side of the arch.

"Because son." His voice was always deep and steady. "Because we really know nothing of this girl. She is young and maybe foolish, but I tell you, Edward, her eyes are sharp, and if she shook off this fit of piety as young girls do, you'd find her mind sharp too. It is dangerous."

She heard Edward laugh a little.

"I would be glad could she see anything but God."

"She could well see too much."

Merca forgot to listen for a moment, temper she had forgotten rising that Edwin should say she suffered but a fit of holiness; she who would give God all the days of her life. Calming, she listened more carefully. Let him be right about her at least that her wits were sharp. She had known there was something odd about this household.

"In any case, Father," Edward said then, "we have nothing at all a-foot today."

"Nothing?"

"Nothing. Manfred and I go to stare like all the other gawpers. There will be other times, but not today. Besides," there was a note of something obstinate in his voice, "I would like to take her."

The father hesitated before he answered, as though he considered something new.

"Well then, take your sisters too."

She heard Edward's grunt of disapproval. I insist.

"Very well then, sir."

They had gone then, and Merca little wiser.

She went back in to Gundred in the hall, and dutifully dropped a civil curtsy.

"Madam," she said. "I will say my prayers at home. There will be no time to go to the minster before Edward takes me to see the king ride into Westminster."

"Do you think that you would like this, child, who have been so anxious not to go about before? The crowds will be large and noisy, and you will grow very tired."

Some cool obstinacy rose in Merca.

"It is time, Madam, I think I saw a little of London. I have been foolish enough to stay so much at home."

Gundred looked baffled and annoyed, but what could she do? The girl was right. All these past days they had been annoyed with her because she would not go out. Now she was annoyed with her because she would. Certainly it was not fair, and it would attract more attention if she made a scene. Besides, Edward said there were no plans abroad today.

Merca watched her walk away, and then, filled with guilt and contrition, she hurried off the sunlit court to the silence of her chamber, falling on her knees beside the bed.

God had gone from her. Try as she would no prayer would come—nothing but the words of Edward and his father, following each other through her head and telling her nothing; the words of his mother, who was clearly annoyed that she could not keep her from going to see this Norman king. And pictures of Edward with his deep, intent, gray eyes, smiling his pleasure that he should take her abroad in London.

She found that she was smiling too, stupidly, at the wooden wall where the sun fell beyond the bed, listening to the bells beginning to ring all over London, telling the people it was time to gather in the streets to greet their king.

Shaking herself, she looked up at the black crucifix above her head, and then at the sun flooding in through the open shutters of the window. With a murmur of apology and a brief signing of the cross, Merca turned for the sunlight and the open door.

Chapter Six

The sun was gone before they found places from which the girls could see clearly through the crowd that made a dull and silent fringe along the edges of the road, gray clouds gathering from the north as though they too had come to meet the king.

"William's weather," said Manfred darkly, looking at the sky, holding a hand out to the first few drops of rain. He looked then at the people. "They would not come at all," he said darkly, "were they not made to."

He spoke thickly through the purple bruising round his mouth. When he had first come into the house that morning, Gundred and the two girls had clucked around him, full of pretty sympathy and soft words. Manfred told them he had walked into a stable door, creeping round his father's stables after curfew. Merca watched and listened; heard their pity and their laughter, and knew it in her bones as a small play acted for her benefit, so that she herself might not ask him what had happened.

Over their blond heads, Manfred looked at her with bright brown eyes, and she at him, and silently he asked her not to speak. Now in the chilly wind that crept along the river, she stood in the thin crowd of sullen Saxons and wondered what it was that she was shielding. The impulse that had driven her to come out this morning had faded into shyness. She had too long avoided the company of her own age, and she walked stiffly beside the others in their high holiday spirits. They cared not one jot that William was coming back to London, but the day was a holiday, and Constance flirted happily with Manfred, her gown of rose red wool picking up the high warm color of her Saxon face, her fine veil blowing round her pretty hair. The small Mary bounced along at Edward's side, tossing her long braids and clinging to her brother who kept firmly close to Merca, threading a way for her through the gathering people.

They came to a halt along the river bank beyond Westminster, where Merca had never walked before—where the river curved beyond the minster, beyond the palace gates and the man with the dancing bear; where even the peddlers with their small hot cakes and ripe red apples, ceased to pester.

"You will be able to see here?" Edward asked her, and she nodded. Why not, for they were on the edges of the very road itself, soldiers strung thinly here, as though William had no need for fear until he reached the center of his capital.

Manfred and the two girls had turned toward the river bank behind them, and Merca found herself alone with Edward. As the night before, she did not know how to ask her questions gently, nor wait to find things for herself.

"What," she asked him abruptly. "What happened to Manfred's mouth?"

Edward looked down at her, her head very little short of his own, so tall and light she was. He knew his father was right. She was so fragile-looking that his fingers ached to trace the lovely bones beneath her fair freckled skin, and to hold the thin fine hands that he might feel their shape. And shy; given she said, to God. Yet the eyes in the thin face were bright and sharp. And they did not smile enough. Now he smiled at her, and did not ask her to believe him.

"You heard him," he said. "He walked into a stable door."

She made a small cluck of annoyance.

"And you too," she said. "You ran into the minster seeking sanctuary from a stable door!"

Gravely he looked at her.

"Yes," he said. "It was chasing me."

To his delight, the simple jest succeeded, and her quick sudden smile lit up her face. He almost stammered, in his pleasure.

"I have never seen you look like that before."

"Like what?"

"You smiled. You were—different." He could have told her how different, but he was learning that one word too much, one easy compliment that would delight his sisters, could close her instantly to cold unhappy silence.

William was a disappointment to her when at last he came.

"I thought him tall," she said. "I thought him tall like all these Normans."

"He is but middle height," said Edward absently. "Robert his son is even shorter."

"Is the Duke Robert there?"

Her face was almost eager as she craned on tiptoe to try and see all the faces that passed her by in a rush of hooves and a flutter of cloaks and pennants; at their head the thick strong figure of the man they had begun to call the Conqueror; dark red hair above a strong, inimical face; a purple cloak, and pale eyes flickering over the silent crowds who stared and stared and would not cheer him.

"Duke Robert comes little to this country," Edward said. "Those are his two other sons. Rufus with the red hair, and Richard, the fair one."

She wasted a moment glancing at him, caught by some note of cold hostility in his voice. She would like to have seen Duke Robert, whom Queen Margaret admired so much—a man of peace who, like the queen herself, thought kings had no need to rule forever by the sword. Quickly she looked back at the cavalcade that was already almost past, catching only a glimpse of red hair and fair, and then of a familiar broad and stocky figure.

"Look, Edward!" she cried, and did not realize she used his name. Kings forgotten, he turned to her in sudden pleasure. "Look, there is King Malcolm."

"Thus I had seen," he said, and did not take his eyes from her. "You care for him?" he added then, curiously, seeing her face alight with the first true warmth he had known on it.

"He is the husband of Madam my Queen," she said, and looked after the vanishing band of horsemen, behind whom the people were closing across the road, blotting them from sight. She could not say what sudden pleasure it had given her to see King Malcolm, as though some small part of Scotia had been laid into her hands here in this far place.

"They are, you see," she said to Edward, and slowly then fell silent, her big eyes searching his face as though to ask him help her say the things she felt. They are, you see, she wanted to tell him, not like other people. She wanted to try and tell him what she had tried to tell Dag, that they were not like a king and queen who held chill state together and knew nothing else. She wanted to tell him somehow of the love and tender warmth that filled the court of Scotia, because of this big man and his beautiful, adoring queen and their flock of small handsome sons. But she could not, gripped, even as she tried to say it, by the same cold tongue-tied agony of shyness in which she would fly from the sight of her king and queen together, their love plain upon their faces.

Fear. More than shyness. Sick fright that took her again now, looking into Edward's close concerned face. Why was she here, her prayers and duties left aside; Manfred in front of her with an arm about each laughing girl, Edward beside her, putting a hand beneath her elbow to steady her in the jostling of the thickening crowd as they came toward the city? These things were not for her.

He could not think what had happened. What had he said to bring back this cold frightened face? She was shivering now, trembling under his hand like the small fledgling he had picked up this morning, fallen from the nest above the warehouse door. Quickly he seized on this; on anything to get her back; for she had left him.

"I found a little bird this morning," he said. "Fallen from its nest. I climbed up and put it back. Do you think that it will live?"

She did not hear him.

"He does not fight, you see," she said carefully. "He is a good king because he does not fight. There are no more wars in Scotia. Only with the men of Moray, and this my lord had to do to hold his throne. The queen has taught him to hang up his sword."

He was bewildered.

"Malcolm?" he asked, trying to follow her thoughts.

Earnestly she nodded, calmer now that she had found something she could say that would thrust aside all talk of love. But she moved away from Edward, chill and stiff again, her hands in her sleeves and her head bent into her hood against the fine rain. He did not understand her, but some instinct told him he must keep her talking. That if he could only keep her talking, he might grasp some straw to help him know what troubled her. For something did, behind this composed and flower-pale face.

"Is it good," he asked her. "Is it good, do you think, that King Malcolm hangs his sword up in this way. Of what use is a king without a sword?" Though the good God knew, he thought as he said it, that England would be a happier place if this William had been less ready with his own.

She could not tell him why it was good that kings should turn their backs on war. She had told no one, not even her beloved queen, more than a few words of what could happen to two children when a king reached down his sword and buckled it about his waist. She did not want to tell anyone. It was enough that she was safe with Queen Margaret, and that Malcolm rode no more to war. In the closed silence of Kilrymont, where the world could never reach, she would be safer still. But although she would tell him nothing, she felt some strange urgency to give answer to this boy. It was like explaining something to herself.

"We rode," she said, as though it answered him clearly. She was breathing hard with some dreadful effort. "We rode down through Northumbria," she said. "Where your king had been with his sword." She could not tell him about the memory of the path along the forest that was like a wound hurting her head, and she did not know why. Fiercely she thrust it away. She would not think of it; would not think of it. Would not think of it.

Edward's silence made her turn her head and look at him, and his face startled her from her own obsessive thought. Straight ahead he looked, as though he were alone, and his boy's face had vanished, hardened into a cold ruthlessness that would not sit ill on the Conqueror himself.

"I know," said Edward viciously, "I know, and all England knows, where the Conqueror has been with his sword and his torches and his branding irons." He looked about him then. They had reached the place where the road turned into Westminster and the path led off across the causeway to the minster. Merca had stopped, and the holiday crowd had flocked on past—no one close save the few devout padding the causeway stones to the great church, and the small black coots splashing with their thin scarlet feet in the edges of the river. The rain was heavier, wide silver rings on the quiet water. The boy leaned close to Merca. He must speak whether he should or not. "There will be those, I tell you," he said, and she barely knew him for the smooth and civil Edward. "There will be those who value England enough to see to it that soon the Conqueror will hang his sword for good."

She looked at him in amazement.

"But the king," she said. "His wife," she said, and then began again. "I mean," she was stammering in her difficulty to tell him what she meant. "I do not hear that the Lady Matilda is like to our Queen Margaret. Would she teach her husband to leave his wars?"

By love, she wanted to say. By love, and love alone, like Queen Margaret. But she could not say it. Edward did not need her to.

"Madam Matilda?" he cried. "Beautiful and hard and bright as the gems in her own crown. William would take no heed of her. Oh, no," he said then, "we were not thinking of asking William to sheath his sword."

She was very quick, catching the word "we."

"Someone would kill him?" she asked sharply, and he nodded, grave eyes on her face.

"You would kill him?"

"If need be!"

She was silent.

"And is that not the reward of tyrants?" he asked. "Of a foreign tyrant who has taken the throne from a Saxon king?"

He had said too much, and knew it. Were his father to hear him, he would take a whip across his back and rightly so. There was something about this quiet girl that made him want to tell her everything—that nothing would have value if she did not know about it. But he must tell her no more, no more. Sweat started on his face that in some foolishness he may have misjudged her. She could go straight to Malcolm, who could in turn go to his liege lord, William. And they would not kill him quickly; or his father, or Manfred, or any of the others. Fear crawled into the pit of his stomach, and he felt the flesh move underneath his skin as though it shrank already from agonies he could not imagine. What had he done?

Merca lifted her long heavy lids and looked at him, and he thought any death worth while if she would only stand there until it came, dark eyes wide and quiet, and the mist beading the soft tendrils of her hair.

"I have tried once to do it for myself," she told him, as quietly and sedately as she might tell him of some new stitch in her embroidery.

"Tried to do what?" he asked her.

"To kill a king," she said, and from some dark place in her mind came the echoes of it. "I have tried myself to kill a king."

Her eyes were steady on his speechless face.

"Malcolm," she said.

Manfred and the two girls seemed like a hundred people, running back along the road to find them, their laughter sending the small dark birds scuttering for shelter on the water lilies, and turning Edward and Merca to meet them blindly, as if they came unwelcome from some other world.

"I will go now," said Merca quickly, "to my prayers."

He could only watch her back, hooded in her dark cloak, vanishing over the wet stones of the causeway. His sister's eager fingers pulled at him, glad to be rid of the pale-faced prig who monopolized their Edward all the day, and Manfred watched him with bright hilarious eyes. It was something to see the handsome Edward so stricken by a wench!

Mary and Gundred were at home when Merca came back to the homestead by way of the deserted path along the river, through driving rain that washed the courts to mud, and stained the wooden buildings a dark uneven brown. Dougal was with them, his plaid cloak steaming at the fire, and on all three long Scottish faces some silent strain that halted her at the door.

"I am disturbing you, Madam?" She dropped her small curtsy to Gundred and felt the rain run from her cloak onto the floor.

The three strained and anxious faces had been turned toward her as though it were someone else they waited for, and it was Gundred who recovered first, clucking with concern over her dripping cloak and sodden shoes.

"Such a day for holiday," she said, and was already unwrapping the girl from the wet folds. "And where is Ed— where are all the others?"

So it is Edward they wait for, Merca thought. What has

happened? How close was Edward himself to the killing of a king? Closer, probably than she had ever been.

The three about the fire were so anxious that they could not keep silent until Edward came, or Edwin.

"In any matter," said Gundred, and her cheerful face was pale with strain, "in any matter, you are coming too, so you may know of it."

"Coming where?" Merca looked from one to the other, and Dougal and Mary spoke together.

"To the court," she said.

"To the Norman court," said Dougal, and Merca frowned a little.

"Why Madam," she said then carefully, for she would not show she knew one word of Edward's mind. "Why are you distressed? Madam my Queen said that it was possible we might be permitted to attend once upon the king."

They were all silent, for they could not answer her.

"There is much, dear child," Gundred could have said, "that Madam your Queen does not know." And burdened with Gundred's secrets, that were her husband's and her son's, Mary and Dougal could do no more than keep silent too. Edward came soon, looking as Merca had done from one face to the other, his eyes in the end resting on her still with clear amazement, obviously longing to continue their conversation where it had been broken off. But he was alert too to the gray fear on his mother's face, and he came back to her.

"There is trouble?"

She shook her head.

"I don't know." She glanced at Merca. "I don't know, Edward. We have been bidden tomorrow to wait upon the king. We and all our guests."

Edward blinked and his long deep breath could be heard through all the silent room.

"It could mean nothing," he said at last. "My father is a man of wealth; perhaps they know his worth."

Faintly the mother shook her head.

"The girls too?" asked Edward.

She nodded. "Where are they now?"

"With Manfred at the cock pit."

"We cannot refuse?" the mother asked then.

"We dare not," said Edward, and, as though the mother felt suddenly that she had said too much, she rushed into explanations to the silent Merca that there was no concern; it was merely that no Saxon was at ease in William's Norman court.

"We must wait for your father," she said bleakly.

"Will I go and get him from the warehouse?" Edward asked.

"No, no!" Stark fright was clear on her face for a second. "We must not let them know the command disturbs us." Then she composed herself, remembering Merca. "It can wait," she said, "until he comes."

Edward glanced at the girl beside him, her vague and other-worldly look completely vanished; alert eyes flicking from one to the other, and he half opened his mouth to tell his mother she need have no caution. He had told Merca already more than he intended. And she had told him more than he had ever dreamed.

There was no time to talk to her before the evening meal; the whole family keeping close together in careful calm and conversation, united against some unformed threat.

Edwin was late, coming in soon after the girls, the shadows deepening toward curfew before they heard his horse clatter through the stable yard. The brave determined evening greeting of his wife did not deceive him, looking from one to the other of the silent, waiting faces.

"Something is wrong? There is trouble?" he asked as Edward had done before him.

"Husband, we do not know." Gundred's fingers were creasing and uncreasing the folds of her gown, belying her calm and careful face.

"Edward?" he said, and the boy answered him.

"Father, we have been summoned, all of us, to William's court tomorrow. All of us, and our guests."

"And think you, Edward," said Edwin calmly, "that the Conqueror does us honor?" Almost he smiled, and the tension eased about the quiet room.

"No sir." Edward smiled too and his grin was broader.

"Then we are all in danger!" Gundred could not hold her words and looked at once in anguish at Merca. Edward put his arm about his mother.

"Do not heed Merca," he said. "She is more any of us than you may know."

There was not time for explanations, only Mary looking at the girl as though she faintly understood what Edward meant.

"All of us," Edwin said then. "Son, how can they harm all of us when our guests are in the company of Scotia's king?"

Edward shook his head.

"Father I do not know," he said urgently. Even as he spoke, curfew boomed into the falling dark, and one and all fell silent until it had stopped.

"I do not know," Edward went on then, "and it may be you are right, they will not harm the others. But you and I, good Father. You and I. That is another matter!"

They were another family from the gay and laughing group that had splashed their way along the sunlit river. They stood close as though it gave them strength; no tear even from the youngest girl, but dark fear in all their eyes as they faced what they had always known. That it might someday come to this.

"But why," Merca cried suddenly, standing alone beyond the fire. "Why does he not send his men to take you here."

She felt the palms of her hands cold and wet along her skirts; familiar fear creeping like an insect through her brain; soldiers twice her height with swords as tall as Dag. Taller soldiers now, with spears above her head. Desperately she begged God not to let her show that she was frightened. If she were right in what she thought of Edward, then these fair girls with their quiet faces had reason to be just as terrified as she.

As if he noticed suddenly that she stood alone beyond the fire, with all the family grouped to face her, Edward moved from his mother's side and came across to her. She saw the mother's eyes grow for a second sharp, noting what he did.

"All of us," he said then, "in a crowd, and who will see the few that vanish, dragged like fish upon a hook out of the crowded river! William is tired of threats against his life. He-would pretend now that his kingdom moves toward peace, that Norman and Saxon lie down together, and welcome him as king. He no longer makes public those that prove him wrong. Though they may be many," he added viciously. "The rest of you may well be sent back here as though nothing has occurred."

His father looked at him below heavy brows and had nothing to add to what he said.

"Manfred?" he said then.

"Manfred," said Edward. He looked at the food grown

cold upon the table, fat congealing on the roasted lamb, and the hot bread sinking in the baskets. "Eat your meal," he said, "and I will go to Manfred."

It was Merca beside him who started, a hand laid upon his sleeve.

"Curfew! It is after curfew."

Quietly he looked down at the long thin fingers, and touched them as though she had given him some splendid gift. Instantly shy, she drew it back, but he spoke to her alone.

"Curfew?" he said lightly. "Does Norman William think he can hold me at home at night because he rings his little bell?"

Danger left the room and death drew back. Edward grinned reassuringly around them all, and lifted his hand.

"I will go to Manfred."

CHAPTER SEVEN

The atmosphere had changed in the high-raftered hall. Fear crept out from shadowed corners like the hungry dogs who sniffed food abandoned on the table. Close together, the father and mother sat wordless, waiting for Edward to come back, and the two girls drew to their sides, fair faces pale and still with terror they barely understood. As long as they could remember, they had listened to talk against the Norman king; had known that in some way Edward and Manfred were always on the edge of danger, and they must never ask them why. The sun had shone and the summers come and gone and winter grown gray above the river, and Edward and Manfred had safely come and gone themselves. Their mother had been always there, calm and cheerful in their absences, and their father too, presiding at the family board as though he never counted up the numbers round it.

Now in an instant there was uncertainty and fear, no easier to withstand because they did not know exactly what they feared.

Merca knew. Quietly and carefully she sat herself upon a stool near Mary, as though by being close to this one breath of Dunfermline and the world of safety, she might manage to be calm. Out of all of them, she knew best the vengeance of an angry king.

"Sir," she said to Edwin, her words as tight and difficult as the twining of her fingers in her lap. "Sir, why can we not all go as soon as curfew lifts to Malcolm our own king, and ask him to shelter us."

Dougal stopped his pacing up and down the floor between the dogs, and laid his hand on his sister's shoulders.

"I'd not think," he said, "that *we* are in danger. It is not us that William wants. But if King Malcolm were to shelter Edwin and above all Edward, there would be war. No doubt, there would be war."

"I would not have it." His face quiet, the father's voice was clear and calm. "I would not have it."

War. Nor I, said Merca's mind, and it was as though the inside of her head began to shake. No war. No war. Like a phantom of the very word, Dag's face came up before her, and the queen's, bent above her in the cold sea wind. Then suddenly Edward's, in clear painful detail such as her eyes had never admitted.

"No war!" she shouted then aloud. "No war!" and did not know that she had spoken, and in the startled silence while they all stared at her, who had never more than murmured, Edward came back like a shadow through the door. Abruptly Merca stood up, and as he came into the candlelight, his eyes were first for her.

"Manfred too," he said then to his father. "Manfred too, and his parents. Others too, that he has had time to ask. All of us, no doubt."

"He would have done as well to come and take us in," the

mother cried again, and once more Edward shook his head.

"No, no, I tell you, he pretends now there is no disaffection in his kingdom. No one will notice this way, but I tell you, every bolt hole out of London will be stopped." He paused and some of the strain left his young face, the same grin creeping over it as Merca had seen in the minster, when he and Manfred, light-headed with their escape, had given saucy answer to the prior. "At least," Edward said, "all the bolt holes William knows will have been stopped."

No one answered him, and looking round their strained and frightened faces, his grin faded. If he knew anything that William didn't, then it was their only hope of safety, and mutely they begged him to tell them what it was.

"I have a plan," he said, and took a stool beside the table. He picked up a piece of bread, and only then looked over the uneaten food, and round them all again. "You would be wise to eat," he said to them quietly, "for if my plan is any use, I would not know when the chance will come again."

His father joined him at once, coaxing Gundred and the girls, and Edward spoke again only when they were all about the board, hungry suddenly with hope, and the thought that food might help them into safety.

"It is us they want," Edward said then, as Dougal had said earlier. "We who have been plotting against William. Another month," he added bitterly, "another month, and we would have been ready." He turned to Mary. "As soon as curfew lifts," he said, "Dougal will take you back to the dwelling where he lodges with all the Scots, and you will take Merca and my sisters."

"My sister?" Mary asked then, and reached for Gundred's hand.

"She must leave. She is of our house."

Gundred's eyes moved to her husband's, and beside them the small Mary began helplessly to weep. Edward made a movement of impatience.

"It will not be for long! We will go, Manfred and I, and you my parents, before dawn."

"In curfew!" his mother cried, and Edward nodded.

"When the Scots ride home," he said "we will be waiting on the road north. There are always spare horses, and who will notice a few more among so many? William will never know that we have sought shelter in Scotia. Malcolm will never know," he added.

Hope ran among them like flame through a fresh thatch.

"It is possible!" cried Dougal and Edwin nodded carefully.

"King Malcolm rides for Scotland on the first of May," said Mary breathlessly, and Edward looked at her.

"That I wanted to know," he said.

"But what, son," Edwin said then urgently. "What of the time in between"? There is a month."

"There are places," was all Edward would say.

"Can I not know where my sister is," asked Mary, her mind full of vague plans that if it all should fail, then Queen Margaret might help her search for Gundred and her husband.

"If you do not know, then you can tell no one," Edward said, and reading their minds, he added, "They will not trouble you, I say. You are under the protection of the King of Scotia, and William would be too proud, the stiff-necked bastard, to ask Malcolm to help him keep his crown."

They were comforted, but Edward moved restlessly on his stool.

"Cockcrow is close," he said urgently. "We have need to plan."

"We are in your hands, my son."

He shot his father a glance, and of the two his young face was for a moment older.

"I will find cover while we wait," he said, "but the road north is long, and we must know somewhere that it runs that is sheltered. We need to watch for them in safety."

Merca's eyes were on him, clear and sharp and thoughtful, and she spoke almost before he stopped.

"The place," she said urgently, "the place we halted to eat, and washed our faces in the stream. Before the great minster at Saint Alban's. There is a little bridge, remember, where they could hide and still watch the road!"

She felt all their faces turn to her in frank surprise, and shrank back, coloring with dismay, to have spoken out and brought all their attention on her. But, she still thought fiercely, it is a good place. He should be safe there, to wait as long as need be. She did not notice that her only thought was for Edward.

Dougal spoke into their astonished silence.

"She is right! There is this small bridge at an angle to the road. No one would see you—save those who looked."

"How do we find it?" Edward cried, and Mary and Merca and Dougal looked one at the other. In that flat land there had been many bridges over slow quiet waterways. How to tell Edward which one, that he and his parents wait not hopelessly or dangerously in the wrong place?

"It were well," said Dougal, and then, "But I could not."

They looked at him, their food forgotten again, drooping from their anxious hands.

"I was going to say that I would go with Edward, and so know the bridge. It is a little off the road. But I dare not. That would be helping William's enemies, and I am Malcolm's man. It would be war were I found with them."

The father nodded, and did not see Mary look suddenly at Merca, who looked back at her and without one word began to tremble, closing her teeth to stop them chattering in the silence—her big eyes, dark with terror, turning then to Edward, who said no word either but leaned upon his two hands across the table pinning her with a steadfast gaze that begged her for an answer.

"No!" she wanted to cry, and could find no voice to break her silence. "No, no, no! I am afraid! I have known it all before, flight and terror and starvation and pursuit!"

But no sound came. Edward, watching immobile and waiting for what she would say, could himself have wept for her, his young face torn with compassion. For she would be brave, he knew. No matter what it cost her, and the cost was clear in her pale face. When all the others had despised her, she had caught his heart at once with this strange fragile dignity underlying all her priggish manners. Brave she would be.

"I will come with you," she said.

Edward only smiled gravely, and laid a hand in a gentle gesture on her cheek. For the others, the cries of astonishment and doubt, and the quick easy tears of the women. For him, she had said only what he expected.

They left in the pitch-black hour before even the first bird stirs with fluting promise of the dawn; the night full of silence and wet river smell. Tide was ebbing yet in the utter quiet, not a wavelet stirred to slap against the jetty.

There was little talk, and Edward forbade it utterly once they were outside the house; away from the weeping girls about the dying fire, after the solemn blessing of the father, who lifted his fair head and looked just once and long about his raftered hall, as though he never hoped to look at it again. The mother was calm and quiet now, turning firmly from her daughters that she might give them strength, bidding them calmly to see to it that when she met them at the bridge they were neat and tidy as befitted those who rode in the company of a king. Only Merca, close beside her as they left the lighted hall, saw the dark anguish of her determined eyes, and knew the cost of her calm words. She slid a thin cold hand into Gundred's arm.

"I will care for you," she whispered. "I am good at living wild."

Gundred stared and did not understand, but squeezed the chilly fingers.

"You will hold close to me," said Edward. "Close so that my every step is yours. The others know the way to the boats as well as I do. You could make a noise that would betray us all."

He had not been idle in his hours away. A boat lay below the jetty, rowlocks wrapped in sheepskin, immobile on the quiet water, no more than a darker shadow on the black river. Every creak as they climbed in was like a sword thrust, and every whispered word a shouted invitation to the Watch to come pounding off the streets. But no sound disturbed the black silence as they pulled out into the stream, wrapped in the night like a cloak, curiously distant and estranged from the squares of candlelight in Edwin's hall; nothing to concern them now except their own wordless care that they should not make a sound, listening in anguish even to the murmur of the muffled rowlocks and the soft whisper of water about the blades.

To Merca it seemed almost as though they themselves had vanished. From her seat back in the stern she could see nothing, no shadow even against the utter dark, all faces hidden in the hoods of cloaks. Only the even thrust of Edward's hands into her sight and out again, told her that she was not alone; that the whole thing was not some dream of terror from which she would wake in her warm colored bed in the tower at Dunfermline, to the Queen Margaret and her loving morning greeting; to the small princes and the king. Like a small, clear, loving picture of some distant landscape, she thought of Queen Margaret and her huge adoring husband, walking as they were wont to do, together along the green lip of Dunfermline glen. As though they were there alone in a world belonging to none but them. She found herself gently smiling, and then her mind stumbled into confusion. Always before, she had felt uncomfortable before the happy love of Malcolm and his queen, frightened by something she did not understand. Now suddenly she smiled, and did not know why she had changed. Abruptly she moved, to disturb thoughts too difficult, and Gundred hissed at her from further up the boat. In the blackness, Edward turned suddenly from his oars, and she caught the quick white flash of his reassuring smile.

Before dawn, they were in the reeds, and Merca watched them grow like spears around her against the paling sky. Between them blazed the first rose flush of dawn, doubled in the quiet water, and the wild geese rose in troubled clouds from the coming of the dark boat.

Edward watched the birds, beating off into the sunrise, honking like a call to arms.

"Fools!" he said. "Fools," as though they had been people. "Do they want to alert the whole of London? We are not that far yet!"

"How far are we, son?" asked Edwin, and Edward threw

back his black hood.

"Far enough anyway to have no need of that. Here we will be seen or we will not. It is luck. If some fellow looking for a good duck for his pot shall come this way, then we are finished, unless we spot him first."

He caught the expression on his mother's face.

"Good mother," he said patiently, "whom do your daughters need most? You or some fellow with a bow and arrow in the reeds." He did not wait for an answer, but spoke again to his father.

"If you have courage to stand up, you will see we are not long beyond where Royal William builds his London Tower. But we have reeds and marsh enough to cover us while we make quiet way to north and east, where I can find place to hide until we take the road north."

He turned then and looked at Merca, long and tenderly, all pretence abandoned that there was not now something special lying between them.

"All goes well?" he asked her, and for the first time she freely smiled at him, so that Edward, startled, lifted his fair brows almost to his hair.

"So!" he said approvingly. "You must do that more frequently."

Fear seemed to have vanished with the darkness. Their safe passage of the black dangerous river had lifted all their spirits, so that Edward in the end had to warn them to be more quiet.

"The reeds hide us," he said urgently, "but the cheeping of a moorhen in this swamp can still be heard a mile away. You are worse, my mother, than the geese."

Quietly all through the long fair day, they crept through the tall spears of the reeds, Edward giving the oars for stretches to his father, but sitting behind him all the time to guide him through the apparently trackless maze of water.

"And when, my son," he asked in amazement, one time that they changed over places, "did you learn all this?"

"When," said Edward coolly, "I learned to hate the Norman king."

He had small chance to talk with Merca; a whispered word or two with Gundred's eyes on him, when he changed places with his father. Yet by the time the sky flushed once more for sunset with rose and amber and trailing wisps warmed to the same gentle color as the evening sky; her smile had grown soft and easy and her eyes lambent as the deepening light ahead of them above the water.

"See husband!" hissed Gundred, who had missed not one soft glance nor tender smile. "See what is happening beneath our very noses!"

Edwin would not understand.

"I see nothing," he said, "except a splendid lack of Normans. Our son deserves much praise."

Merca overheard, and stretched dutifully over to help Gundred divide the careful ration of bread and cheese that would be their evening meal. She listened calmly, who had hitherto been so shy that one word of criticism would send her into scarlet-cheeked retreat. Nor did she quite know herself what it was that had happened. But now suddenly, since that moment when she had said that she would come with him, nothing was the same. Calm happiness filled her, leaving her untouched by Gundred's frowns. Even fear was held at bay. Warm reckless certainty upheld her that nothing could bring her harm with Edward at her side. Normans! Kings! Danger was no longer real. Reality lay only in the flaming sunset beyond the darkening spears of the reeds, gilding Edward's fair head and turning the dusky marsh into a drowned rose-colored sea, where mallard rocked in brown content and the small black moorhens scuttled from the oars.

Impulsively, she reached forward and touched Edward's belt. Instantly he looked round, bright pleasure on his face that she should have made such a gesture for herself.

"Yes?"

"Surely," she looked round her into the calm silence, broken only by the small lap of water and the last evening cheepings of tired birds. The sun was going and the rose red water fading into steely blue. "Surely," she said, "no one would follow us here?"

Edward's face changed, grim beyond its years.

"You should ask my lord Hereward," he said, and she did not understand him.

Gundred clucked from the other end of the boat.

"And if they do not," she said to Merca's question. "And if they do not follow us, what use is it to us, sitting in a swamp. I have need to meet my daughters on the road to Scotia!"

Gravely Merca looked at her, round Edward's tall back, and pity touched her for the cheerful Gundred who had so gaily welcomed her and Mary when they first came from Scotia. Sitting, as she said, in a swamp, her son in mortal clanger and her husband with him; her loving pretty daughters torn away, and only God in goodness knew if she would ever see them more.

"Edward will care for us," said Merca gently, and knew it wrong. Gundred's unhappy eyes glared at her as though she dared her to know what Edward would do. Poor soul, thought the girl, she has but this one child to cling to now, and surprise filled her at her own compassion, who would never before have understood. She looked at Edward's back in front of her, bending steadily to the oars, and she was filled with a great sudden longing that they should talk, as she had never talked to anyone before. Talk about themselves, about herself, about this new strange happy Merca, who could look at Gundred and know her misery. Like Dag, she thought suddenly. Now I am like Dag, who has always known about other people. Dag. She ached too to talk to Dag. To tell him of Edward. And what would she tell him?

Edward was speaking. While she had been dreaming there behind him, darkness had fallen on the marsh, the final streaks of scarlet day holding the western sky down at the level of the water, a flight of geese arcing white against the last light, their feathers faintly stained with fading rose.

"In a few minutes," Edward said, "we are going to land."

"And may God be thanked for that," his mother said.

"I hope He may," Edward answered, "but you will find little to thank Him for at first."

"What do you mean, son?" his father asked.

"We are in the great marshes," Edward answered soberly. "There are paths, and I know them, but we have a long way to travel before we may hide in safety. There is the marsh all round us, looking for but one false step. And there are the Normans, looking for us."

There was silence, and the last light faded from the western edges of the water.

"Why, my son," asked Edwin, "do you feel so sure they will look for us here?"

Gundred's anxiety was as tangible as if she spoke aloud. "Mary," was all she whispered, no louder than the murmur of water in the reeds, and "Constance." Merca stared in the darkness at the pale oval that was Edward's face.

"Because they look here for everyone now, good father,

since my lord Hereward made The Fens the last stronghold of the Saxon."

"Ah," said Edwin, as though he understood, but to Merca once more, the name of Hereward meant nothing.

The boat thumped gently against something more solid than a bed of reeds and Edward grunted, lifting in the heavy oars.

"Give me the rope," he said, and his father fumbled for it and handed it over in darkness now so thick that they could barely see each other's hands. Edward laughed suddenly, and Merca felt his fingers brush just once about her face, a small secret gesture that she understood when then he spoke.

"If there is a splash," he said lightly, "then it were best pull me out quickly, or there will be an ugly sucking noise as the marsh lays claim to me."

"Edward!" cried his mother, but he laughed again, and was gone past her over the prow of the boat. Merca thought of the day he and Manfred had laughed in the minster, when no doubt they had just escaped by some hairsbreadth from these same Normans who pursued them now, and she felt pity for him, who could not go lightly into this danger, with Manfred, as he had gone before; but must be burdened with two women—his mother weeping with her fears.

"I at least," vowed Merca then, the boat moving to some silent pressure in the thick dark, "I at least, will not burden him with my terrors, no matter what may happen."

He was back beside her before she even saw him come.

"I was lucky," he said. "Found an old stump almost at once. She is secure now and we can sleep."

"Sleep!" cried Gundred.

"Sleep," said Edward firmly. "We have been one night awake, and we have a long way to travel."

"The boy is right," Edwin said to his wife's protests. "We are in no hurry. If he says we are safe to sleep here, then safe we are, and will travel better for some rest."

"Safe?" Merca whispered to Edward. "Are we safe?"

He felt strong and confident beside her in the darkness, against the dying grumbles of his mother at the far end of the boat. She sensed him rumble with laughter.

"Unless the tree give way, that I tied her to," he said.

"And what then?" She could not help smiling too.

"Then," he whispered, "the tide takes us as it comes up the estuary, and brings us back all the way we came, and up the river to lay us at good William's Whitehall steps like pigeons trussed ready for his pot!"

"And we still all asleep!"

"And we still all asleep!"

Gundred could not bear their smothered laughter, insult to all her terrors and anxieties, and even while Merca laughed into her closed fists, some part of her own mind went wandering amazed, to know where her own fear had gone.

"Come child," said Gundred firmly. "Come, Merca, you shall come down here and sleep with me. Edwin, you have the stern with Edward. We shall sleep better thus."

They touched each other's fingers in passing in the middle of the swaying boat, and above them the first faint stars marked the black sky with silver.

Chapter Eight

The next days and nights were like a deadly dream haunted by the sound and sight of water; great shining sheets of it with birds rising in clouds against the glittering sky; steel gray masses of it, with rain driving dark into their faces over flat endless marsh with never hope of shelter; green oozy marsh water, lapping their sodden shoes on the thin treacherous paths that Edward showed them; deep dark pools where a man might drown in a thousand times his depth, and barely have the space to fall. Endless water; the soughing, lapping sigh of it, and the cold wet smell of it. Often Merca paused and looked about her, at the endless wastes of what seemed half of land, broken by nothing but the bending reeds and an occasional wind-torn tree. What in God's name, she would wonder, would they do here without Edward, whose feet unerringly picked a path from the sea-ridden land, where no track seemed to lie. Back behind her she looked and on ahead; nothing but the glitter of the marsh pools and the tall watching reeds, stretching to illimitable sky. What in God's name would happen to them if his memory should falter?

At each blazing sunset that stained the whole huge arching sky with agonizing beauty, he found for them some small patch of higher land; some little island untouched by the rising tide, and here they would huddle into cold, uneasy sleep, wakened again by a dawn as brilliant and encircling as the sunset. They spoke little now, as though the very effort of unnecessary words might hold them back in the long cold struggle to they knew not where; Edward first, then Merca, holding tightly to his cloak; then the parents, the father plodding steadily in the rear to encourage Gundred who paused increasingly and looked about the empty trackless world in something like despair. Then clearly she would think of the children waiting for her on the road to Scotia and to safety, and put her eyes again on Edward, as though in him lay her only hope. As it lay for all of them. Edward himself was calm and endlessly good-tempered, often looking round to smile back at Merca, clearly bidding her to wait, that their time of talking was yet to come—their time of happiness, everything that mattered to them, was yet to come, his brief secret smile said to the girl behind him, her numbed fingers clinging to his sodden cloak. Frequently, he would turn and take her clasping fingers gently away, while he went back to help his mother over some dangerous place, holding her raw terror at distance by his steadiness and calm quiet.

"My son, how long?" Edwin asked on the second night. Even he looked gray and shaken, tired by the long heavy-footed trail, sapped by the cold wind piercing from the open sea. "My son, how long?"

Merca had taken over the food, untying the bag from her shoulders where Edward had tied it to try and save it from the wet. Curiously, it seemed as though all life in-between had vanished, as though she had spent all her living days a fugitive, groping in some meager parcel for enough to eat. Panic struck her suddenly that this was all; never to be otherwise again. Then she found Edward's eyes upon her, and he sat down close to her on the green soaking grass, as though he sensed her feelings.

"I fancy a small capon," he said to her, and his gray eyes held her with love and steadiness. "Well roasted, with a suckling pig to follow." Then he answered his father. "Little longer, Father. Little longer. By noon tomorrow we shall be where I want to take you." He spoke again urgently to the relief on his parents' faces. "But do not think I lead you to much greater comfort than you have here. Only the same as my lord Hereward knew, and that is good enough for us. The journey after that will be easier."

Merca blinked above her small ration of bread, and sipped her share of the water Edward passed her. The lord Hereward again. Whenever in this bitter life that time came for talking, she must ask him who this was. She half tried to frame the words at once, but she was too tired, too cold to make the effort; pale weary lids drooping over her eyes as she slid gently over to Edward. "Lord Hereward," she mumbled, and he put his arm around her; pulling her close for warmth and whatever comfort he might give her; torn with pity for the small windflower face, blue with weariness and cold. Thin pale face, fragile as this tiny flower, and yet what was this that she had said to him—"I tried to kill a king." He was as urgent and desperate to talk to her as she was to him. What king and how? Malcolm, she had said, but how? So thin and light and frail, yet she would kill a king?

Amazed he stared down at her and longed to talk, but his mother's tired, frightened eyes were on him, and he held his peace, doubtful now of her courage if they should run into trouble. If she knew nothing, either of him or of the girl, then there was nothing she could say. A pang of pity touched him for the bright cheerful woman she had been, taking all danger for granted when she faced it from the warm safety of her husband's hall. Crumbling now on the edge of hopeless terror. He leaned over gently and touched her hand.

"Sleep now, my mother," he said. "Sleep now, and tomorrow you will be safer."

His father's red-rimmed eyes warmed on him, and they looked at each other in a long moment of understanding, as though Edwin had spoken aloud, and said to him: "They are indeed ours, my son, and we must care for them. She is yours and your mother is mine, and we must do our best for them."

He eased the cloak around his wife's shoulders, and her gray head went down on his, exactly as Merca's had done on Edward's, and the two men in silence watched the dark night creeping in across The Fens.

The next morning was indeed better, but brought with it its own fears. The land seemed a little firmer, easier to walk on, and over beyond the soft streaks of the sunrise, it seemed to rise a little, a gray blur on the endless flat horizon.

"Ely," said Edward to their questions. "No, we will not go there, for the Normans have it now. They took it from my lord Hereward in the last battle; they have dispossessed the monks and driven them away, and the people live in closer curfew than all of England. The Normans do not trust The Fens."

"Ely?" said Merca. "The Fens?"

"The Fens." Edward waved a hand around the glittering morning marsh, sun in the wide waters and reeds bending like dancers in the wind. "The marshes. And Ely is an island that rises in the middle of them. Once, they tell me, there was nothing here but sea."

Edwin smiled with the wry good humor of a few hours' shivering sleep, his lips cracked by the salt wind.

" 'Twere better that way now, my son, and we could have kept our boat."

He was startled by the vigorousness of Edward's denial.

"No Father," he said urgently. "Were it possible to take a boat, my lord Hereward could never have held out as he did. Were the Normans fifty paces over there"—he pointed to a green level-looking patch of grass—"they could never reach us, unless they knew the paths. If the reeds allowed a boat, then they could come straight across."

"Edward." Merca could wait no more. "Who is my lord Hereward?"

Edward blinked at her, and even the parents looked shocked.

"I forgot," the boy said then, "that you are come from Scotia." He looked round the empty wastes of reed and water and his face grew sad. "They called my lord Hereward," he said then, "the last of the Saxons. He was not, of course," he added, "for there are such as us, who would follow in his steps. But he was the last to give serious trouble to William, whom he defied for years among these reeds and swamps. The monks of Ely helped him, and for this the king threw them from their monastery and took all their possessions."

"And now?" Merca asked. "Where is he now? Dead?"

Edward shook his head.

"No," he said. "Our Norman William is too clever for that. Were he dead, then we could hate him for his death. No, William makes friends with all his enemies. My lord Hereward is heaped with Norman title and rides on command of William's army. He is too clever too, you see, to waste the most brilliant soldier of his realm."

"Perhaps," she said urgently, "the king may be lenient to you if he should catch you. And Manfred."

Edward touched her face gently for its look of loving faith, and shook his head.

"It is only the important he makes friends with," he said. "We are for slaughter as idly as the deer in his new forest."

Gundred caught the tender moment between them.

"Come," she said tartly, brisked like Edwin by her few hours sleep. "We shall never reach this safety unless we get on our way."

It was Gundred then who first saw the Normans, too frightened to scream, standing gibbering with pointing finger to where the long column marched, apparently on the water itself, the morning sun bright and threatening on shield and helmet, sparking off the moving armor and the wide blades of their spears. Merca looked and felt the old sick fear crawling through her brain. Spears taller than a man. Dag. At least Dag was not here. Only she need care for herself. Not yet in her fear-closed mind, had the idea taken hold that now there was someone who would care for her. Then she felt Edward's hand, firm and strong about her arm, and for a second, curiosity drove out fear.

"But Edward," Merca said. "Edward, they are walking on the water!"

Edward seemed to have no care about them at all. Cheerfully he laughed, and, turning, patted his mother's arm to calm her terror.

"True," he said. "They are a long way away," he added, "and could not reach us, even if they wished. They are on the causeway to Ely. King William built it to reach the strongholds of Hereward the Wake, and for four years, every stone that William built, Hereward and his men tore down.

But William," he said sadly, "had more men."

"The Wake?" asked Merca. "Hereward the Wake?"

"It seemed he never slept. No Norman could catch him unawares."

They watched in silence the long column of bright bobbing armor passing apparently through the reeds themselves, and each one of them felt the brave defeated presence of the Saxon who had fought to keep The Fens for England. The Wake, thought Merca, and it caught her mind; ever watchful of his watery kingdom against the foreign king. Hereward the Wake. The reeds were closing the soldiers from her sight, and she did not realize that she had watched them without fear.

The fact that they could see the Normans at such close quarters, and know themselves safe, lifted their spirits for the last tiresome hours of the journey, when the water vanished and the open sky, and the tall reeds closed in walls along the two sides of their narrow path; taller even than Edward, who had need at intervals to tell them to wait while he took his knife and hacked their passage through.

Edward had already told them that they were near the end, when they heard the movements of other people in the reeds, a soft insistent rustling that must also mark their own passage to anyone close by. Edward stopped, lifting a halting hand, and turned back to them, listening, gray eyes dark now and dangerous as the shadowed water underneath the reeds. Faintly it came, the dry rustle of the reeds pushed one upon the other, and, even as they listened, it drew closer. Merca's eyes were on Edward's, ready to act on his smallest word, fear touching her again like the cold eerie brush of snow. Behind her she could hear Gundred begin to chitter, and Edwin hushing her with urgent words. Edward flapped an irritable hand at her, and turned his head again to the progress of the sound among the rushes, and Merca saw the tension leave his face. But when he beckoned them to follow on again, it was with utter caution, a finger laid tight against his lips demanding silence.

It seemed half the journey once again that they crept soundless through the green-brown walls, conscious all the time of the close passage of people not as cautious as themselves. Here and there they heard vague words, and Merca noticed Edward tense again to listen, but he did not stop until they came into the open in one of the many small clearings of green marsh grass that broke the forest of the reeds.

Now he was half smiling, watching the reed wall from where the noise came ever closer, and holding out a hand to the others that clearly bade them wait a moment. On another track further over in the clearing, the reeds broke apart once more. Gundred screamed and Edwin thrust himself in front of her; but Merca had been watching Edward's face and did not move, any more than he did himself, standing with a broad delighted grin to face Manfred's start of shock.

"Were we Normans," he cried then, "you were as good as dead! There is not a wildfowl left undisturbed for thirty rods, for all the noise you made!"

Manfred was too relieved to care.

"Were you Normans," he said, "you would be far from the first to have troubled us!"

They banged each other on the back in frank delight, thus far safe with their difficult journey. Manfred's parents followed him from the reeds, and Merca felt the tears rise hot and salt to see the two gray-haired women so far removed from everything that was their lives, embracing each other in this strange lost world of reed and water, their hair dishevelled underneath their cloaks; their sodden kirtles girded to their knees. Not only children, she thought. Not only children suffer at the hands of kings.

Manfred turned and gave her his bright warm smile as though they met happily in Edwin's court.

"You came a different way?" she asked him, and he gave a shudder at the memory of his journey.

"We came out of London to the north," he said, "and then across the country. It was a mistake. I think every Norman not busy bending at the knees to William was out after us." His quizzical face crumpled, and he ducked his head toward his mother. "And my lady mother is not made for flight."

Merca could not but smile too, to where the round plump figure of Manfred's mother disengaged herself now from Gundred, and launched into a torrent of words about their dreadful, dangerous journey. Swiftly Edward stopped her.

"Good wife," he said, "you seem to have some idea that the danger is all over. You can be plucked from these reeds by the Normans as easily as on the road. Let us, I beg you, keep going."

She gave a small whinny like a frightened horse and gathered up her skirts, prepared to charge the reeds alone. Firmly Edward placed her beside his mother in the line, and bade Manfred go to the end of it. One last pleased grin they exchanged as he went, and from behind him Merca tweaked Edward's cloak.

"Edward," she said reproachfully, "that surely is not true."

She felt him shake with laughter, and knew a surging lightness of spirit that the two boys were again together. Nothing seemed so woeful or so dangerous now.

"What?"

"That the Normans can take us as easily here as on the road!"

"Of course they couldn't," whispered Edward. "What of Hereward? But I know Manfred's mother, and if once she starts to talk, then we are here till sun-rise."

Like sheepdogs at the front and rear, they shepherded their unlikely flock through the last tired hours of their long journey.

The first that Merca knew of its ending was the strange unearthly creeping sound of men's voices singing—whispering eerily through the darkening reeds in a plain chant now long familiar in Dunfermline. She heard Gundred exclaim behind her, and the wordless gasp of Manfred's mother, but the boys urged them on.

"Edward!" She pulled again at his cloak. "It is Compline."

"Yes," he said briefly. Compline. The last office of the monks' day, the evening prayer of the church that asked peace and blessing for her children for the night. Every evening she heard it in the candlelit quiet of the great new church where the monks were, down the hill at home. At home. So much a part of all she loved and longed for, this sad uneven chanting that punctuated all their days. Now it crept with a strangeness fit to chill the blood through the tall stems of the reeds, between which night was already come, only the bright lambent sky above their heads telling them that elsewhere it might still be day.

Suddenly, with no word of warning, they walked back into the light. Out of the reeds onto an island larger than any they had seen in all their journey, stretching off green and flat into the dusk, dotted with reed-built huts of every size, and with the green flickering fires of salt-soaked wood. From over to the left came the haunting chant of Compline, and from around the fires figures rose like shadows, and Merca caught the red glint of spear and sword blade.

"Edward!" she cried, and he laid a hand on her arm.

"Be still," he said. "Let them come close enough to see us."

Manfred held the others quiet and, as Edward had said, the moment the armed rush was close enough to see them, standing with the sunset on their faces, the weapons fell and the bright evening was filled with shouts of welcome. There was not one of them had more than rags to hang about his body, and their gaunt faces wore the stamp of half starvation. Nor were the ones singing Compline any better, when they came to the end of their office and filed from their corner of the island to join the others who crowded about the newcomers. They were, if anything, more gaunt and terrible than all the rest, yet carrying their rags and hunger with some grave incomparable dignity.

"Edward," whispered Merca as they came. "Edward, who are they?"

"They are the monks of Ely," Edward said. "Dispossessed and banished by William, to go back to their monastery on pain of death. Here they have held out ever since; and still hold out, even now my lord Hereward is gone. They say he presses William for their pardon."

He moved forward and knelt to kiss the ring on an old hand so emaciated that it was no more than bone and shriveled yellow skin.

"My lord abbot," he said. "I have friends who need shelter for a while."

The keen, ancient eyes roamed over the small company, taking in without surprise the two sets of parents and the staring girl.

"You did well to bring them, Edward, Manfred," he said.

"They must all be precious to you."

They did not look any better in the morning, when all the company of the island, after drilling with their arms along the green soft grass, sat down to care for their small supply of spears and swords and arrows. Merca watched them, honing their weapons in the fire; fitting new feathers from the wildfowl to their ragged arrows; damping and testing the fine balance of their bows.

"Edward," she said, as he came up beside her. Now she never waited for him to speak, as though all the years she had been so quiet had piled up words that must now come tumbling out. "Edward, it is not so easy."

"What is not so easy?" He barely listened to what she said, intent only on looking at her, more beautiful than ever now that she was not so pale and overtidy; her cheeks warmed and flushed by her good night's sleep; her hair unbrushed and unbraided these many days, tousling round her face in soft curls. He did not care what she said, just if she went on talking. "What, my love?" he said, and she did not notice the endearment.

". . . Not so easy," she continued urgently, "to kill a king."
Now she had all his attention.

"Tell me of it. Tell me of how you tried to kill a king!"

Her mind was still on the men working on their weapons. "You see, they have been here for years, trying all that time to kill King William, and they have not succeeded. And you too? You were trying to kill him, you and Manfred?"

There was no point now in secrecy. He would get her confidence for his. He nodded. "But we are so young. Still, had we time we might have succeeded. But they caught on to us."

"That day at the minster?"

"We had a secret place we used all to meet, down below the wharves. Someone must have told. They rushed us, and caught two. That no doubt is the reason for the call to William's court. The ones taken will have talked."

They were silent a long moment, facing in their minds the horrors that simple statement covered in William's Norman England. They would have talked that they might be allowed to die.

"But we are safe now," said Merca urgently.

"I think so," Edward answered. "By the time we travel again, the hue and cry will be died down, and we can get to Scotia without attracting much attention." Then he turned to her and looked again at the narrow fragile face. "But you," he said, "what have you had to do with the killing of a king!"

She shook her head. "I was but a child. I thought all I needed was a bag of gold, to hire a man to kill him."

"Tell me," he said, but still she hesitated—still held by some dumb difficulty in talking of any of these things that had happened when she was a child. Gently he took her hand, sensing her great need to talk; the need that in itself made it so hard for her.

"Tell me," he said. "I might get some hint for killing William."

She laughed then, as he had intended and, first in a stumble, then in a rush, came the long foolish tale of how she had hated Malcolm because he had overrun Northumbria and left Dag starving and without parents or a home.

"It was not myself so much," she said earnestly. "I did not matter, but Dag could not live alone." The calm self-contained image of her brother's face came up before her. "At least," she corrected hastily, "I thought he could not live alone. And he did not remember Christmas. All this I thought Malcolm had done to him, and I hated him. I hated him. Dag did not remember Christmas." She paused, breathing unevenly, and Edward kept silent lest he stop her. Only the bare poor bones of some dreadful story this, and the greater part of it not told. *What matter if Dag did not remember Christmas when he might die of hunger,* he thought. But to her, it mattered, and he must not stop her. "Then Queen Margaret found us, or Mary did," she went on, "and took us to Dunfermline, and it was only then I found that she had married Malcolm."

"Ho!" said Edward, and tried to soften the poor strained face. "Living off your enemy, eh?"

But she would not smile.

"Yes, yes, and I tried to take Dag away, but he would not come."

"Wise Dag," thought Edward. "I must know this Dag."

Now she was talking of someone they had met on their hungry travels, called Thomas the Knife.

"All he wanted was a bag of gold and he would kill anyone, even a king. But he wanted a lot of gold for a king."

"No good to us," said Edward, but still she would not smile.

"I thought all I had to get was the bag of gold. I tried to steal it." She stopped then, saying no more for a long moment. "Then they took me to Iona, where they bury Scotia's kings. It is across the sea. Very beautiful, Edward." For a moment she kindled. "The islands lie like smoke drifting on the sea, and all the cliffs turn rose red in the sunsets." She stopped again. "I saved his life there," she said abruptly.

"You *saved* his life!"

Her voice was flat now, as though no one could believe her story, nor even she at this time understand all it had meant. "Someone else had paid Thomas of the Knife. He woke me, going to the king's tent, and I followed him and thrust away the knife."

Edward had nothing to say, staring at her in blank amazement, trying to assess how much more went on behind that quiet face. Then she turned and looked at him, her great eyes dark and direct upon his face, filling him with some splendid hopeless weakness, so that he could only go on looking at her, wordless, waiting for what else she had to say.

"You see," she said, as though it explained the whole long story. "I had learned to love King Malcolm, although I did not know it. After all, he was Queen Margaret's husband."

"Yes," said Edward. "Yes, my sweet, I see. You no longer had need to kill a king."

She shook her head, and tenderly he looked down at her, his young face touched with pity.

You learned to love the king, my poor pretty, he thought, *because he was married to your beloved queen. And you love this little brother, Dag. But unless I am mistaken, when you first came to London, you had not yet learned to love anybody else. That was why you were bound for the convent."*

So long he looked at her, silent in his own thoughts that she shook his arm.

"What is it, Edward? What are you thinking?"

He took the hand from his arm.

"Only that we will be a peaceful couple," be said smiling. "You no longer want to kill a king, and now I wouldn't dare."

Then he let her go, and asked her no more. But he knew there would be more to come. More grief and horror somewhere still that had sealed this lovely girl into her own shadows in her mind; leaving her running from the world, love only given reluctantly to one person here or there. It was up to him.

"She learns already," he told himself hopefully. "She learns already."

Chapter Nine

Edward promised that the journey from the Fens to the road north would be far easier.

"We are safe enough, away from London," he said. "Now that a little time has passed. In London we had been seen, Manfred and I. They knew who they were looking for."

Merca nodded. They stood at the edge of the reeds, waiting for the older people to finish their farewells and thanks to the good monks and their fighting men, who had so gladly shared all the things they sadly lacked themselves. She looked in silence across the green island, so flat that at high tide it could seem lower than the sea itself—a strange, lost, secret world among the rushes, inhabited by men all driven by a dream. Always she would think of it as she had first seen it, lapped by the darkening sea, dancing with the blue-green flames of drift, and Compline creeping from the night.

"I have been happy here," she said suddenly, and Edward smiled at her.

"And I," he said, and knew quick, delighted pleasure that he had been the one to make her say this. No word of love had yet been used between them, and yet he knew her happy because, on this hidden island, she had brought herself to trust him; telling him at least some of the sore bitter secrets that still haunted her. Words of love, these, although she did not know it yet herself.

Gundred came with some of her old spirit from these last words with the abbot, her dignity restored by his. The others followed, and Manfred came silently from behind them in the reeds. At the water's edge, the monks and their little army gathered to say farewell, bones and weapons alike sticking through their rags, clinging to their citadel of a long-lost cause; sending the small party with their blessing out into a world where they themselves had been forgotten.

They left the marshes and made their way unwatched and unmolested across the fair, green, summer country, working by the sun to where the old Roman road must cut the country north and south.

"And your task comes when we hit it," Edward said to Merca, and she nodded. Odd, the things you came to be grateful for. She could not know herself now for the sour, speechless girl who had ridden down that road, but at least her silence and misery had not allowed her to distract herself by chattering. She had nothing else to do but watch the road, and could remember every step of it.

"South," she said confidently, when they came out at last onto its beaten tracks.

"You are sure?" Edward asked her, and Gundred began to fuss, pulled to the pitch of her nerves by the hope that soon she should see her daughters once again.

"South," Merca said, looking at the quiet sunset above the

dark woods, so calm after the flaring scarlet skies above the marshes. "To my left hand." Suddenly her hands grew still as she gestured, and she held them and stood looking at them. "That was another thing with Dag and me," she said then to Edward confidingly, as though they were alone. "I did not know my left hand when Thomas the Knife told us which way to go."

He took the poor confused hand in his and held it. Please God, let her tell him all, and everything, to rid her of these painful ghosts that haunted her. He felt convinced that, if only he could love her enough, somehow that would reach her troubled mind and set it free.

"Merca, Merca sweet, it does not matter. You know now. Which is your left hand?"

She crossed herself and then held out the hand whose shoulder she had touched first. Manfred roared with laughter.

"I would know," he said, "by putting up my fists. I lead always with my left!"

"When I was a child," said Gundred suddenly, "I used to suck my thumb for comfort. I knew always it was my right thumb. So I knew my right hand from my left!"

They all stood in the middle of the dusty road, and chattered in sweet relief that the worst part of their escape was over. Safety should be here on the morrow or the next, with Malcolm's train of followers, spare horses, and cover on the long ride north. Edward watched the tension fade from Merca's face as she laughed at Manfred's capers, punching an imaginary enemy in the middle of the road that he might be sure of his left hand.

By the sunset of the following day, it seemed their anxieties were ended. They were riding in the tail of Malcolm's train, reunited safely with all those they loved; well mounted and well guarded—the long, cold, shivering journey through the marshes receding from them like some distant dream of terror.

With the coming of safety, Gundred reasserted her authority.

"Merca, child," she said firmly, "you shall ride with me and Mary and the girls. Edward, take your place among the men."

"Yes, good Mother," said Edward meekly, and tried to resist the amusement on his father's face. He could not resist Manfred doubled up with laughter behind him.

"And leave that girl alone, Edward my son," he cried in high falsetto. "You are not old enough to think of girls!"

"Ah, Manfred, friend," he said when he stopped laughing. "It is no jest."

Manfred's dark eyes turned on him, deep and sensitive and heavy with affection.

"And what is, my Edward," he asked. "The Normans? The Fens? Death? Love is just something that you must fit in."

Edward shook his head. "No longer, Manfred. No longer." He searched for words. "I am more conscious of her needs now than of my own. Her life is more precious than is mine." Her needs. When could he talk to her again, and let her talk, with his mother standing dragon all the way to Scotia? And indeed what then? They had thought of nothing other than to get safely out of London, and keep their heads upon their shoulders; now it seemed there was a future. Merca was the ward of the Queen of Scotia, who by all accounts was said to be more perfect than the Blessed Virgin. What would she make of him, coming penniless and workless to her court? And could he even stay there, hot from his plots on the life of the English king?

At the moment there was nothing he could do to resolve anything, save to ride patiently with the other men, as close to Merca as he could be; she in her turn trying to ride in the rear of the company of ladies, so that when they stopped at roadside streams for water, or to take short rests in the high heat of the day, they were able to exchange a few secret words that said nothing other than that every hoofbeat on the road to Scotia made them more certain of their love. They were content to wait.

They came in the light of a brilliant evening, up the long, gentle, sloping road toward the rebuilt inn where they had stopped on the way down. As she realized where they were, Merca half turned toward Edward, disturbed by some immediate unhappiness.

"What is it, sweeting?" asked Mary at her side, aware of the change in the girl's face. Since they had met again, Mary had been very tender to her; as she had been when she was young and first come to Dunfermline.

"I thought her a prig," she had said remorsefully to Gundred. "Now I think she was for some reason just unhappy. I was not good to her."

Gundred said nothing. She knew what had brought the new smiles to Merca's face and, ward of the Queen of Scotia or not, she would want to know a great deal more of where the girl came from before she would deem her fit for Edward, son of the most prosperous wool merchant in London. She had forgotten in her recent safety, that her prosperous wool merchant was riding cap in hand, an exile from his city, to hope for charity and protection from Scotia's queen.

Now Mary looked anxiously at Merca's suddenly pale face.

"What is it, sweeting?" she asked again, and Merca turned back, staring at her with blank dark eyes that focused nothing.

"The innkeeper, you will remember, had no ears," was all she said, and privately Mary thought that she should be grateful she and all her friends were riding safely north, and not themselves cut into little pieces in some black dungeon of the Norman king.

"These things happen in war," she said, without great thought, and then shrugged. Merca was not listening, lost in some private world, and looking, Mary thought unhappily, like the tight-faced girl who had ridden down this way. Behind poor Dougal, she recalled, who had not got a word from her from Dunfermline down to London.

Not only Merca now was turning around. The whole bright colored column halted and shifted suddenly on the narrow road; turning their horses; turning themselves in their saddles, frightened listening faces coming against the blank stares of those who had heard nothing.

"What is it?"

"Horses!"

"A column!"

"The Normans!"

"The king! The king!"

Clearly, above the panic cries of the women, came the harsh thunder of hooves, pounding behind them up the long slope they had just traveled.

Fiercely the men cried for quiet, beating the horses into line; shouting at the foolish women that if it were the Normans then what of it, it was naught to do with them. Among the quietest and the most willing to move back into line were Edwin and Gundred, and Manfred's parents, quick desperate glances telling each other that if by any chance this column was on the search for trouble, then the less attention they brought to themselves the better. Around them, the women chittered into calm and joined them, until the column was moving raggedly again toward the north, scouts gone flying ahead to Malcolm where he pressed on for home, despising the shelter of the inn where the women would spend the night.

Merca alone remained, standing in her stirrups facing backward down the slope, jostled and scolded by the other women turning back into the line; her eyes fixed on the dark dust cloud thundering toward her up the darkening road—above it, the last low sun taking sudden flurries of bright color, caught from a streaming pennant or a polished lance. The women had passed her before she even moved or spoke, and Edward was already kicking his horse toward her from the men behind.

"Edward!" she cried then, hoarsely. "Edward, Manfred! Follow me!"

They did not wait, conscious as she of the speed of the approaching soldiers, and the impossibility of breaking forward through the press of frightened women huddling like hens across the narrow road.

Almost beside them, there was a path off along the edges of the wood, that on the journey down had beguiled and beckoned her and in the same voice threatened her with terror. Now she knew that down it there could be a chance for safety. No time to wonder how she knew. Faintly she heard the men shouting at the women not to follow them and then she was alone, flying along the beaten path. Behind her she could hear the hoofbeats of Edward and Manfred, and the noise on the road growing shrill and distant; about her, darkness thickened in the silent woods.

In a small clearing she at last drew rein, and turned to look at them, panting behind her, their eyes on her and all their faith in her. She had brought them here.

"Merca," said Edward urgently. "Do you know where you are?"

For a moment he despaired at the wild blankness of her eyes, certain that she had done as he feared, and fled blindly from the column in a panic. Audibly he groaned, and Manfred's good-natured face turned to exasperation.

"In God's name!" he said, "we are worse off than if we had stayed. Malcolm at least might have helped us.

She looked at their faces, pale and desperate in the dusk, and her own cleared.

"He would not," she said coolly. "He could not. But I can. Yes, Edward I do know where I am." It was as if her whole mind broke suddenly into light, where there had been only dark and fear. "Turn loose the horses." She had slid to the ground from hers, even as she spoke.

"Turn loose the horses!" Manfred was aghast.

"I can hide you," she said. "I cannot hide a horse. We can get others if we can get to the inn safely by morning."

She could feel the two boys staring at her in the green cool gloom, as though she were some ghost risen from the mosses at her feet.

"I told you," she said, "that I knew where I was," and as Edward thumped from his horse, she took his hand. "This time I shall lead you."

His teeth shone white for one bright smile, and then he led the two horses off to the clearing edge, giving them a good bang on the rump to send them off into the woods.

Manfred still sat obstinately on his.

"You can move faster on a horse," he said.

"Well then, I beg you," whispered Merca, "move fast away from us." She felt Edward's amused and admiring glance on her that she should speak thus to Manfred. "A horse," she went on, "in the woods at night, makes noise fit to wake the dead." She paused a moment. "Wake the dead in stone coffins. That's what Thomas the Knife said."

Edward almost groaned again. Thomas the Knife, whoever he was, had no place in their desperate situation. He hoped she knew what she was doing. "Come Manfred," he said peremptorily. "Get down off that horse or get to the devil on it."

Manfred shrugged and got down.

"On your head," he said.

Edward had the faint feeling that Merca was walking like someone asleep; her hand in his leading him quietly and steadily deeper and deeper along small woodland paths, that must clearly have once been in constant use, yet would be difficult for any stranger to locate in the thick brush that grew below the trees.

"You have been here before?" he asked her in the end, and he felt her hand tremble slightly in his, but she did not answer him.

Behind him, Manfred crept along with expert quietness, still grumbling softly about his horse.

She stopped at last, when in the fallen night there seemed nothing ahead of them but a green wall of undergrowth, rising like a rampart underneath the trees. Too like a rampart, Edward thought. Something man had made. She was ahead of him then again, forcing her way through what might once have been an arch, but was now no more than a thin place in the solid wall of clutching briars and brambles. A thin, cold moon was rising, showing them into a small open space that might once have fronted to a homestead; facing a dark broken shape that might once have been a house. Secret in the woods, dark as the trees themselves, lost in the rampart of brambles.

"Ah," said Manfred behind him, and Edward knew him right. "As safe this as The Fens, to let the present pursuit pass by."

"It is well?" asked Merca, her voice curiously dead.

"It is well," Edward said. "But we had better get inside."

It could no longer be described as a dwelling, holding only the memory of a house in its collapsed thatch and crumbled lintel; formless, and filled in the darkness with faint whisperings and rustlings of creatures who had lived here so long that people were forgotten. They pushed aside the creepers growing over the gap that had been a door, and Edward felt in Merca close beside him some sick reluctance to put a foot on the sunken stone that must have been its threshold. Wild with curiosity, yet desperate for their safety, he put an arm about her waist and gently eased her through, feeling all her fear and horror in the stiffness of her body, and her fast uneasy breathing. But in his circling arm, she bent below the tangling creepers and went in.

Only darkness inside; nothing to be seen, and nothing heard save the sightless scurrying of small frightened creatures, but even Manfred sensed that to Merca this was no casual hiding place, chance found by fortune in the forest. The silence between her and Edward cried louder than the mournful hooting of the hunting owls around them in the trees, and almost before he was through the door behind them, he said hastily, "I think it wise that I keep watch outside."

They did not even answer him, Edward groping in the thick darkness for Merca's shaking hands. He did not have to ask her.

"It was my home," she said, in a cool, small, dreadful voice. Edward strained to see into the pale oval of her face.

"Tell me, Merca," he begged her. "My dearest, tell me. Tell me everything."

He saw her head turn in the direction of the door, and heard her breath draw hard and bitter as a sword thrust.

"There," she said. "There across the door, my mother lay. We had been in the forest with the pigs, Dag and I, and the Scots came with King Malcolm." She paused and then went on, her voice grown hard and strained as though she could barely find it, but must or never find herself again. "The thatch was on fire. I looked in past my mother. My mother, my mother." She began to weep, deep desperate sobs of grief held all the years and never understood. Edward held her close, tears helpless in his own eyes in the darkness, crooning as he might to his own small sister in some childish grief, stroking the long silk of her hair.

"Tell me," he whispered, close against her poor tear-wet face. "Tell me. Tell me."

And she did; how she had looked past her mother at the door and what the soldiers had done to her mother's body; past her mother to where her father lay. "And Edward," she whispered, "he had no head. It wasn't there. And there was blood, blood, blood all over everywhere. I screamed at Dag to go away. I would not let him see. I took his hand and began to run. We came at last to a road, I suppose it must have been the inn, poor man," she added, and Edward's heart lifted to hear the thought of someone else, "it must have been burned twice. There was no one there, only the inn burning and it was almost dark and we went on up the road and on and on and on. I did not remember on the way down. I suppose I didn't want to."

She was beginning to relax against him, and slowly, piece by piece, the whole long tale came out, as she had never spoken it before, even to Queen Margaret—all the horror followed by the grief and fear and the deep desperate clinging to little Dag because he was all the world had left her.

"And in truth," she said suddenly, after a pause, "I know Dag was better able to manage than I was myself. But you see," she said simply, "I had to feel Dag needed me, or I would have died."

"And I had to hate Malcolm, I think," she added after another long pause, "because I had nothing else to do but hate. There was no one left to love. Except Dag—and he could not remember Christmas." She told him of the distant bells that told her it was Christmas night, and Dag could not remember.

"Somehow that was worst of all," she said, "worse than being hungry or cold or anything else." She paused again, and he could hear the sobs easing from her thin body, and her breath growing longer and steadier. Hate surged within him, for anyone who had brought her to such trouble, and then wearily he let it go. What was the use of hating; she Malcolm, and he William, and if it were not them, then it would be someone else. One might as well take kings as they came, for God knew there was little to be chosen between them. Merca spoke again.

"When I learned to love the queen," she said, "I found I had learned to love Malcolm for her sake. That was why I couldn't kill him. But—"

"Yes, my poor, my lovely," Edward whispered. Everything that haunted her must come now, or there would be no future for her.

She seemed to find it difficult again, breathing hard against him in the darkness, as though her very thoughts distressed her.

"I know now," she said painfully, "that I had not learned properly to love. Enough only to keep myself content. I could not love the world as I was growing up. That was why I wanted to go off into the convent. I think love frightened me. Perhaps I thought if I should love, then some king would come again and take it all away. I used to be frightened and unhappy to see the Queen and King Malcolm walking together, so happy and so much in love. So were my mother and my father. I knew that even though I was so small. So happy."

She was weeping again, but this time quietly, as though from very weariness of living again in this short dark hour all the agony of years. Edward took his cuff and in the darkness wiped away the falling tears.

"Enough," he said gently. "Enough. We are done now with tears, you and I. And with kings. We shall find a small homestead for us and our children, and live there far from kings and wars." And he added: "We will let the kings live too, and trouble not our necks in trying to kill them."

He sensed her smile, and in the darkness pictured how her pale lovely face must look, smiling gently with these great eyes drowned in tears.

"Oh Merca," he said, and held her so close, wrapped in his arms as though he would protect her from all the world to come, as from her griefs long gone. "Oh Merca."

She lifted a hand and placed it on his cheek.

"Edward," she said then amazed, "you weep yourself." He did not answer. "You weep for me? For me?"

"Who else?"

Behind them where the door gap showed the paler light of moonlight, the creepers rustled and they heard Manfred's urgent voice.

"They are coming," he said. "I hear them. They are searching the forest."

Chapter ten

It seemed impossible that they would not be found, crouching together in the darkest corner of the ruin where the smell of time was dank and cold and heavy with decay. Fiercely Merca closed her mind to all thoughts of what had once been there, that she might not betray them all by screaming out to Edward to take her away from this place; now that she had raised about her ghosts that for years she had managed to forget.

Edward held her firmly, knowing her thoughts. Clear from outside in the forest came the sounds of search; of beaten undergrowth and feet thrusting for themselves a path among the brush; harsh voices speaking French, and armor chinking above the soft chirruping of troubled birds.

"Bastards, like their king," muttered Edward, unable to hold his tongue, "that they will speak only French."

In the utter dark, Manfred felt for his shoulder and laid a hand on it, hushing him, and in silence they listened to the search grow close and gradually fade away. So overgrown the ruined dwelling that not even under the clear moon, did the searchers see it as they passed.

Into the new quiet, they drew long deep breaths, and asked each other what was best to do.

"I think," said Manfred, "that if they are safe past for the moment, then we are best to bolt for the inn, and the rest of the company. We are less conspicuous than we would be alone, and they will not search twice in Malcolm's train."

Merca smiled at the faint blur of his face.

"Not if I know Malcolm," she said, and felt Edward's pressure on her hand, sharing the small joke.

"They might come back," he said.

"We'll wait until it is almost dawn," said Manfred. "They'd not come back after that long, surely? Then we can catch the others as they leave."

They did come back, in the dead hour of darkness before dawn, and through the cracks and gaps in the ruined walls, the flare of torchlight moved slowly.

"Edward," whispered Manfred. "They do not seem to me so many. I wonder are the others still about the forest?"

Edward did not answer, but Merca knew him listening, carefully, trying to mark the noise and know it less or greater than before, troubled as Manfred was, by even the smallest thing that might seem strange or offer hint of danger.

"I cannot know," he whispered at last. "I cannot know." And there they had to leave it, as the first pale hint of gray came creeping from the dark sky and showed them to one another, dishevelled and dirty in the middle of a heap of undergrowth as wild and tangled as any growing outside.

"We had better go," Edward said, "or the others will have left the inn."

Manfred was already outside, turning an anxious listening head from side to side, struggling that he might hear anything above the rapturous singing of the birds, welcoming the new day with none of his doubt and hesitation. He was uneasy, sniffing the air like a hound, scenting trouble but unable to pin it down.

In the end he shrugged and turned to the two others who had joined him.

"Yes," he said, "we had better go." The sooner started, the sooner they would reach the cover of the inn.

The trouble he had scented overtook them when they were on the last part of the path out of the forest, to where it turned to the straight stretch along the edge of it to the road below the inn. There was no sound, no hint of danger, even Manfred beginning to relax and feel it little more than moments before they would be back in the safety of great numbers. The Normans were as surprised as they when they came on them round the slight bend of the path, the new sun sparkling on their helmets, surprise on their dark faces, standing for a long hesitating second. Edward moved first, flinging himself on them with his stave, lashing right and left in desperate effort to hold their attention.

"Run!" he yelled as he charged them. "Run!" "No!" screamed Merca. "No!"

In her hesitation, the second soldier freed himself, and turned toward them. Frantically, Edward thrust out a foot and tripped him, bringing him to the ground in a great jingling of chain mail.

"Run!" he shouted again above it, and this time Manfred did not let her hesitate. He seized her hand and dragged her screaming into the forest; behind them one soldier battling with Edward's flying stave for a chance to reach his sword;

the other struggling heavily from the ground.

Incredibly he did not follow them when he managed to get up. Manfred was now running wildly, whipping Merca along so that she no longer had breath left to protest, dragging her through briars and bramble and over fallen trees until she wept for very pain as well as for the anguish of fleeing thus and leaving Edward to the Normans. She was beside herself when at last Manfred halted, listening desperately against her wild sobbing for any noises of pursuit.

"Hush," he said urgently, but she could not hush, struggling for the torrent of words with which she would reproach him, pulling at his hands even now, that she might go back to Edward. Firmly he turned and pinned her with a hand across her mouth, and listened again intently; the forest was silent. Whatever might have happened to Edward had happened, nor was there any noise of search coming in their direction. Manfred frowned, puzzled, and then turned at last to the girl held helpless in his arm. His eyes were sad and kind and full of pity.

"Merca," he said gently. "Long ago we came to this agreement, Edward and I. If one were to be taken, then the other must at once fly. No heroic deaths helping where help can be no use. Remember the day in the minster? He had left me as we left him today. Then the other lives to carry out our plans."

She was so limp and silent that he felt it safe to let her go, looking at her questioningly.

"I do not think," she said, and her voice was cold and lifeless as the winter river at the bottom of the glen. "I do not think that now Edward would care about carrying out your plans. We had others of our own."

"What plans?" he asked her sharply, not believing that she knew.

"To kill a king," she said, still in the same voice dead with hopeless grief, and slow agonizing tears began to gather in her eyes. She looked back through the trees as though she might even yet run back to Edward; to go with him, even if she could not save him.

Manfred took her hand again. The woods were silent now, but so they had been in the second before the Normans surprised them. There was no time to lose.

"Merca! We must go! There is nothing to be done!"

He could not bear the look of naked pain she threw him, beginning immediately to run that he might not have to look at her. Of Edward himself he did not dare to think. They had faced this day so often that he yet barely understood that on this soft harmless-looking morning, everything this time was real. Edward, if God was good to him, was already dead.

By the time they reached the road, stretching dim and empty through the quiet morning, Merca would no longer even run, her hand pulled silently from Manfred's, who went on alone, not leaving her, but determined that the pain of telling them should not be hers. Behind him she walked slowly now, up the slope toward the inn, and the whole fine morning world lay about her at some vast unreachable distance—shattered already by the pain of living all over again the last terrible anguish of these woods. She had learned to love, and God had let her understand it all for a few pitiful, small hours. Now the bleak emptiness bad closed in again, closing away the sunlit world, thrusting off to a far, half-focused distance the appalled faces of the family who faced her in the courtyard of the inn.

Manfred and Mary ran to her as she came, and vaguely she was aware of something in their faces more than their grief for Edward; some warning that there was no time to give.

One face stood out before her among all the rest, as Gundred rushed toward her, Edwin plucking desperately at her sleeve, the two girls weeping wildly by her side. The older woman's face was twisted to a mask of rage so bitter and so wild she could not even speak, flinging away her husband who would have held her back from the pale and silent girl, mouthing abuse with hideous half-strangled sounds that would bring out no words. In the stunned misery of her poor disbelieving mind, Merca groped to know why she should be so angry, her cold hands limp in Mary's, who herself wept silently and hopelessly for what had happened and what was yet to come.

"They didn't want him!" screamed Gundred in the end, and her face was scarlet in her rage and grief, wet and hideous with tears. "They didn't want him! You killed him! You killed my son! You killed him!"

She would have struck out at Merca had Edwin not forcibly held her back until her rage collapsed in bitter desperate weeping, but Merca had not moved even with the flailing fists before her face, only turning appalled mute eyes to Mary at her side. Hopeless, Mary nodded. She must know, and she must know now.

"The Normans were not interested in such as Edward," she whispered, and would have bargained her soul away from God not to have to be the one to say it. "Had you stayed with the column, all would have been well. They were searching for some important prisoner escaped from York, and knew exactly who they looked for. Not for Edward or for Manfred."

Clear as though he stood beside her, she heard Edward's voice.

"We are so young," it said, "once away from London, we shall be safe enough."

And she in her panic had rushed him from the road, and

led him to his death. Her eyes turned then on Manfred and he answered her unspoken question.

"Yes," he said heavily. "The search in the forest would have had nothing to do with us."

"Dear my God," she said then, and it was all she said. She felt the very flesh seeming to shrink on the bones of her face, and her limbs shriveling like her heart, that she might make herself as small as possible to let this awful truth pass by. But it would not pass. It lay there in the loving concern in Mary's eyes, touched by the horror that filled Manfred's on her other side. It was in Gundred sitting on a mounting block in the splendid morning, weeping her heart out for her only son; Edwin beside her grown suddenly an old man; the two girls hopelessly comforted by the other women. It lay in the careful withdrawal of all the rest of the party, going quietly about their business for the journey with averted eyes; leaving the others to their grief.

Worst of all it was in the sweet willful fluting of the blackbird in the old tree above the roof. She had heard him in the evening on the journey down, and he had been but a bird, symbol of the world she had not wanted. Now he told her, in the awful stricken quiet, of all the world that she would never know; all the clear sweet springs and gray snowbound winters of the glen that she would have shared with Edward; all the bright splendid fires of autumn and the small flowers of the summer woods; starlight and sunlight and sunset and dawn and all the colors of the world and his children round her feet. And it was she that had taken it from both of them.

Just one dry dreadful sob she gave for Edward, she, who had that night in his arms wept her heart dry for the parents she thought she had forgotten, and the eyes she turned on Mary were bleak and cold and blind.

"Dag," she whispered then, and did not know she said it. "Dag," but when Mary moved to answer her, and tell her they would take her home as fast as possible, she set her gently to one side, and with slow desperate dignity walked across the yard to where Gundred sat still wailing on the block.

"Madam," she said to her, her voice thin as the wind in the reeds. "Madam, I am sorry I have killed your son."

Gundred lifted her head and screamed at her, but Edwin laid a band on her shoulder and looked into the girl's blind tearless face, his pity for her as great as his own grief.

"My daughter," he said. "I think he was yours as well as ours."

For one unguarded second she looked at him, her agony laid bare so great as to touch her eyes with madness, then she veiled them again and thanked him with the same intolerable dignity.

Nor did she lose it through all the long unbearable journey back to Scotia, where the court had already moved for the summer months back to the palace of Dunfermline. Mary watched her, deep with pity. She might at casual glance have been the same silent, difficult girl who had ridden almost without speech all the days of the journey down. But that girl had been dull and almost sullen; now she moved with calm civil poise that was in itself a nothingness.

"Madam," said Mary urgently, when at last she reached the queen with her sad responsibility. "Madam, she frightens me. It is almost," she did not want to say it, "she is almost as though she herself is already dead!"

She looked at Queen Margaret as though appalled that she should hear herself say it, but the queen looked quietly back, her lovely face full of sadness.

"And so I am sure she is," she said. "And for the second

time in her life. My poor, poor Merca. All I had hoped for her came about. I felt that although she might find it hard at first, she was ready to move out into the world. And I hoped, yes, I hoped, that she would fall in love." She paused a moment. "He was good, this Edward?" she asked then, and bleakly Mary nodded. No comfort in trying to pretend that it were better in the end, or any such excuses. Malcolm had come back to her once more, in peace and happiness, more years—please God—ahead, to add to all they already had been given. And Merca had come home alone, all bright promise lost, and filled with guilt that she would carry all her life.

"Because she will, you know," she said aloud to Mary, and did not know she had spoken.

"Will what, Madam?"

"Carry the guilt of his death until she dies herself. It is not in Merca's nature to forgive herself." Mary nodded, and the queen sighed. "Send her to me," she said.

She tried to think of everything before Merca came, summoning the nurse to bring the babies that she might see how they had grown while she was away; bringing the two older princes from their lessons to bid her welcome. But Merca saw none of it, greeting the queen and admiring the babies, kissing the two small eager boys with the same cold, unseeing dignity with which she had traveled home.

"Mother of God, help me," whispered the queen, appalled by the girl's stricken calm that took charge of the whole situation, even of the queen herself, and would allow no word of comfort.

"Merca, come sit here beside me." She patted the bright bolster on the bench beside the window looking down the long reach of the glen. Obediently Merca came, her hands folded in her lap, and the little boys stood apart where once they would have run to her, disconcerted by this strange and unfamiliar Merca.

"Daughter," Queen Margaret began, and was amazed to find herself almost nervous. "Daughter, Mary has told me of all that happened on your journey, but you tell me of it now."

Merca's voice was like the cold sweet notes of a whittled reed.

"There is nothing to tell, Madam my Queen," she said, "there is nothing to tell. We were agreed before I went away that as soon as I came back I should go from here to Kilrymont and join the sisters there. I would be obliged, Madam"—and the cool voice trembled slightly—"I would be obliged if you could arrange for me to go as soon as possible."

"But Merca!"

The dead eyes turned on her.

"Was it not what we arranged?"

Even as she spoke the queen was thinking. It might do the poor child good, to go away somewhere where everyone did not know her story—where everyone would not be looking at her either with pity or with anger for her stupidity. Where she would be safe away from the boy's mother, who by Mary's account was fit to kill her. And that was another matter. She must talk to Malcolm, who had all unwitting brought this load of trouble in his train. This plotting wool merchant and his wife must be settled somewhere well away from Scotia's court, so that William could not pick a quarrel about the harboring of his enemies. Though by all accounts these were but small enemies. Still, William must not have the smallest of excuses.

Now she laid a hand on Merca's still one, cold as winter on this summer day.

"Is it truly what you want?" she asked the girl, and Merca

nodded, her mind whirling behind her silent face. Faces, faces, faces; some of them accusing; some of them looking at her as though she were a fool; some of them finding her pathetic; many, and these were the worst of all, looking at her sick with pity, as though they knew exactly what she felt. As though they knew—as though they knew. Oh dear God in heaven, it may be in Kilrymont she could keep her mind, where the faces did not care for worldly griefs and looked at nothing but God's reflection in themselves. Only among these impersonal eyes who would look at her and see nothing of her; only there might she hope. Hope for what? No more than with God's help to put through each day without beating her head against the stone wall of the tower; leaping at dark from the high spur of the glen; running glad into the deepest pools of the storming river. Running somehow, anyhow, from a life she could barely face from hour to hour.

"Madam!" she cried desperately, and stood up to face the queen. "Madam, I *beg* you, let me go to Kilrymont."

The queen stood too, and put her hands on the girl's shoulders.

"Anything," she began to say. "Anything, Merca, that will help you to be happy again."

But Merca had not heard her, staring past her out the deep embrasure of the window to where a small square figure in a black tunic plodded up the hill, the sun bright on its fair hair and its face lifted to the summer sky.

"Dag," Merca whispered, as she had done in the dreadful moment at the inn. "Dag."

Manners she forgot and ceremony and all conduct proper to the queen's presence, running from the chamber and down the winding staircase of the tower. "Dag. Dag. Dag."

But when she reached him she could say nothing, and Dag who had heard everything, and whose small heart was sick with trouble for her, did not know how to help her, except by being himself.

"You are very pale, sister," he said critically, and Merca looked at him. Not since Edward's death had anyone dared to say anything so simple to her. "London does not seem to have agreed with you."

"London was all right," she said to her surprise, who had not talked herself for days. "London was all right." But she could not go on from there, and Dag did not know what to say next.

"Let us go and sit in our place on the cliff," he said, and Merca thought it like another world; another girl who had been used to going with Dag to a small shelf of rock overhung by the lip of the glen itself—sheltered, secret, overlooking the turbulent river deep at the bottom of the steep ravine.

His very silence helped her, and the long familiarity of the summer glen; crickets shrilling in the long coarse grass and the small harebells trembling in the heather that would soon flush the whole bleak place with transient rose.

"I have learned much while you were gone, sister," he said at last, and tried to find words for the deep excitement of his increasing skills with ink and color that could so surprise even himself who held the brush. He ceased almost to notice her, his eyes rapt on the empty sky beyond the glen, trying to tell her of the great book of the Gospels that his monastery was creating to put into the queen's completed abbey; of the fine dark lettering blazing with the color of the flowers and patterns that twined it round; the little animals; the small foolish pictures that monks put in to please themselves; the color and the gold; the gold. "They are even," he said, awestruck, "even going to teach me soon to use the gold."

He turned at that, to see that she was suitably impressed, and saw she was not even listening. His teeth caught his lower lip in disappointment. How could he help her? This was all he had to give; his little world such as it was. He had no other wisdom to offer to her grief. For a moment tears pricked his own eyes, that he should so love her and come to her trouble with his hands so empty.

"Sister," he began painfully, "I have no words—"

Suddenly Merca turned to him, and laid a gentle hand along his cheek.

"Oh Dag, you have," she said. "You have." And slowly, painfully, as though each word came with its own agonizing effort, she began to speak of Edward, loosed from her locked grief simply by the loved even tenor of Dag's voice, telling of the things he cared for, even though she had listened to not one word.

Dag listened. To the long tale of London growing happy because it had held Edward; of threat and fear and growing love; of pursuit and death that was her fault; and grief and guilt that would stay with her until she died herself. And all told in this slow painful voice that she must find for telling somebody, or lose her mind.

And at the end, he had nothing he could say. Only his blue eyes stared at her in an agony of helplessness. *My good monks would know what to say to her,* he thought, *who are wise in all things, but she would not talk to them and I am only Dag.*

"What now, sweet Merca," was all that he could say. "Will you stay here with us?"

"I am for Kilrymont tomorrow morning," she said, and turned at his exclamation of dismay. "What else is there for me?" she asked him.

Dag groped for words he had once sought before, to ask her why she thought God only wanted her unhappiness. He also groped for some understanding that was beyond him, that more than ever now she should not shut herself away in this dark nunnery. Vaguely he knew that for all her stony grief and her cold desperate dignity, she was not the same priggish sister who had gone away. Blinking he looked at her trying to know where the difference lay, and saw it so suddenly that he exclaimed aloud. Merca turned on him great eyes dark with sadness. "What is it, little brother?"

He could not take his eyes from her. He knew now what the difference was. She had grown beautiful—belonging in one sudden instant with all the passing pleasures of his daily world, like shadow shapes and candlelight and the soft white sweeping of the queen's doves; like the colors of his letters and the gold.

She had grown beautiful, and he could not find words to say so.

Slowly, as many times before when he had failed to help her, he leaned over and gave her one of his rare warm kisses; then he turned and left, climbing steadily up the steep bank to the rampart without a backward glance.

Suddenly he turned and looked back down at her below him.

"And what, sister," he shouted roughly. "What would they have had you do? Ride back and meet these Normans and ask them did they seek your Edward, for if they did you must help him to escape!"

Furiously he stamped on down the hill, brushing at his helpless, angry tears.

Chapter Eleven

They knew nothing of her story in Kilrymont.

Merca had remained silent through all the long ride across the summer moors until they came in sight of the sharp gray line of the sea. Then suddenly, she turned to the queen riding at her side.

"Madam, I beg you," she said with sudden harsh urgency, as though only with the side of the wide bay and the distant huddle of buildings on the red bluff had Kilrymont become real. "Madam, I beg you, tell them nothing of me here. They have expected me long enough, there is nothing they need know."

The queen thrust back the fragile veil that fluttered around her face in the sea wind.

"But Merca," she said gently. "Could they not help you better if they know your grief."

"I do not want their help!" Queen Margaret stared at the furious desperation on the girl's face. Then Merca stammered,

"Your pardon, Madam, that I speak so. Your pardon. It is only, only, that I come here to offer them all that I once did. They need not know what has happened in between."

Because I cannot, cannot, cannot, screamed some silent voice in Merca, raw with sick loneliness for Edward, *I cannot live except with people who do not know my feelings. I can only live with people to whom I am nobody.*

The voice did not have to scream aloud. The queen knew every word it said, and sighed and begged God to have pity on this poor child suffering all that she herself had ever feared to suffer, when Malcolm climbed his great black horse and took himself to war. And yet, with Dag, had he the words, she wondered if it were enough for God that Merca only offered him unhappiness. But she is young, the queen comforted herself. She is young, and she may have been right that the cloister was the life for her. Who am I to be so sure?

Gently she smiled at Merca, and promised her that nothing need be said, and saw a small measure of strain leave the girl's face.

Nothing was said. The queen was welcomed to the hospice on the high cliff above the windy bay with all the love and reverence befitting her holiness and generosity, and the veiled old face of the mother superior welcomed Merca gladly into the community as Queen Margaret's ward.

"There is much to do, daughter. We cannot have sufficient hands."

Merca followed her glance over to a long low wattle building where the cliff sloped down toward the village at the apex of the bay, and saw that from it a thin endless chain of people stretched coming and going, to the small square church built on the opposite bluff. Like ants, she thought, remembering how she and Dag had poked them with sticks to make them run about. Like ants.

"They have nowhere else to go for food and shelter, and you know, daughter, that were it not for Madam here, our queen, they would not have even this. Before we came, many many died that they might see the sacred relics of our saint." The hooded ancient eyes watched the girl's face.

Merca felt a stir of life she had not felt since she had been dragged screaming off from Edward. What was this old woman telling her but things that she already knew. As though she were a simpleton who did not know what she was doing.

"I know, Mother," she said, "all their needs, for I have long lived with Madam my Queen, and learned from her even when I was a little girl to care for those who cannot care for themselves." The spark of life died even as it kindled, and her voice was cool and without emotion, the poor of Scotia as much to her as the ants they looked like.

"And," the old woman said sharply, as though the queen were not there, "did you learn to love them, these poor people?"

Merca's eyes opened wide, and the queen stirred. Enough for the poor child to start learning all these harsh lessons once she was gone. Useless to think we can conceal anything from Mother Gertrude here; she knows more than all the rest of us together. She will soon know everything about Merca.

"Indeed, Malcolm," she said to the king, when she was safely back home into the warm gay shelter of her tower. "Mother Gertrude frightens me." She grimaced ruefully. "I think she knows more than God."

Malcolm growled. Old women ruling the roost in nunneries did not interest him. The pleased look on his queen's face did.

"What did you do?" he asked her, grinning.

His lovely wife gave the gentlest of shrugs.

"I was," she said, "just a little queenly with her."

"Ha!" he said, and grinned again, knowing how his lovely Margaret could shrivel the presumptuous with her gentle dignity.

He looked up from where he taught Edward to bind the feathers to an arrow.

"And why," he said, "were you being queenly with this old woman?"

Now the queen's face grew still and sad, but she would not weary Malcolm with a tale that would not interest him for half way through.

"Because," she said, "because I thought she might be harsh with something she could never understand."

Suddenly she dropped her bright silks into a shower on the floor, and ran across the chamber to him, cradling his great red head in her arms.

"Oh, Malcolm, Malcolm," she said, and he could feel the sobs shaking her, the tears wet in his own hair. Edward stared up in astonishment, and Malcolm set him aside.

"My heart, my little heart," he said, and wrapped her shaking hands in his huge paws. "What is it? What is the trouble?"

The queen was regaining control, breathing deeply, and smiling at him and her perplexed small son through the haze of tears that still spattered dark patches onto her blue gown.

"Forgive me," she begged him. "Please forgive me that I am so foolish."

Still he stared at her.

"But why?"

She freed a hand and wiped her eyes with the embroidered edging of her cuff.

"Because, dearest Malcolm, because you are here beside me. And I have Edward here, and all the others."

"That does not seem to me a cause for tears!"

"No," she said, and went back meekly to her stool, and Malcolm made a face at small Edward as though to ask what should they do with so foolish a mother. Edward grinned back and snuggled up to him, and together they went on feathering their arrow.

Outside in the summer night, the wind blew cold from the east, from the wide sea below the cliffs of Kilrymont, and down the hill in the pale stone church, Dag knelt in his place among the other boys, beside the monks, and found he could not say his prayers.

Late summer came, and warmed the hills with crowns of pink and purple heather, and winter followed them with caps of snow, and gradually Merca found some strange peace in Kilrymont. In the ordered life of the nunnery there was no place for thought, from the first office of the day long before dawn had streaked the edges of the sea with scarlet, to the last prayers by candlelight with the day's work done and darkness fallen; a few brief hours of comfortless sleep before it should all start again. It seemed as though some curtain had fallen between this that was now, and everything gone before. Nothing held reality save cold summons of the convent bells, the ordered prayers, and the endless hours of waiting on the needs of the pilgrim torrent pouring into Kilrymont.

With listless care she gave them food and washed their sores and bound their blistered feet, and listened to their troubles and even learned to offer them mechanical cool words of kindness and comfort she would despise were they offered to herself. Wrapped in their own sicknesses and hunger, and the troubles they had crossed half Scotia to lay before the saint, most of them took no heed of her. It was Saint Andrew they had come to with their woes, and not some neat-fingered silent sister in the hospice, who was but a pair of ears in passing to listen to their grumbling.

Others more wise looked at her as did the old mother superior, and knew her for the husk she was. One old man limped from the hospice door one day, with feet new and neatly wrapped in healing linen, his eyes looking backward at Merca who had tended him. With something close to fear in his old face he blessed himself.

Mother Gertrude was standing by the door.

"Why did you do that?" she asked him, and he understood at once, looking at her with eyes as wise and crinkled as her own.

"Because," he said, "I have been tended by a spirit, and who knows if it were a good one. Heart gone, and life," he muttered to himself. "Only a spirit. God keep us from evil."

The old woman did her best with Merca. She summoned her, toward the end of winter, to her cell of bleak woven wattle, nothing to break its utter barrenness save a black rood fastened to one wall. The ancient nun stood in her hooded habit of hodden gray as bleak and ugly as the room itself. Faintly, as from some other world, Merca could hear the queen's voice crying against those who thought that to be holy, you must needs be ugly. But the voice was faint and far away, coming from beyond the curtain that had closed between her and such life. Now she welcomed ugliness, herself grown thin to gauntness, her great eyes little darker than the deep haunted shadows round about them.

For once, the mother superior sought for words. She was used to gauntness and shadowed eyes, evidence of hard work and little food and smaller sleep, but the starved tired faces of her nuns were usually lit by strange content. They were doing God's work, and offered Him every hardship they suffered in His name. They asked no more. On this girl's face there was nothing. It would have been an easier task had there even been unhappiness. There was nothing.

The queen had been right about Mother Gertrude. Well she knew that this was not the same priggish child who had ridden here the previous summers with the queen, content in her own virtue and feeling that God should be pleased to get her services. That priggish child would have made a poor nun, but she would have settled down, and at least had her own conceit to offer God.

This poor, lovely, empty shell had nothing. Nothing. What had happened in between, that had led her to such tragic beauty, and left nothing else?

Carefully she asked: "My child, are you happy here?"

"Yes Mother." No more than a ghost's voice, as though even speaking was more than she could bear.

"You are determined to stay? You know you are but a novice and can still leave us without reproach?"

One startled flicker of the huge eyes as though they knew a moment of wild fear, and then the girl said carefully, "I am happy here, Mother, and do not wish to leave. I hope I am proving satisfactory."

"Oh, indeed," thought Mother Gertrude. "If we could find anything, the novice mistress and I, that we could blame you for, it might be easier for all of us."

When she saw the girl's cool face the day the queen had brought her, she had thought a few sharp words might shake her into life. Now she knew better. The child was too far gone. They could only add her to their own prayers, and wait for God to help her in His own good time.

She sighed and made the sign of the cross.

"Go in peace, my child," she said.

Merca came out and stood looking at the steel gray sea, the bitter wind tearing at her habit. She was frightened. If they found fault with her, then they might send her away. Here she was managing to live; there was so little to learn; every day the same as every one before. Even she could manage it, but she must be even better than she was. They must have no reason to complain.

In her behavior she redoubled all her efforts, no one more hardworking nor more selfless; more utterly unstinting in her efforts for the suffering pilgrims; more gentle-handed nor more skillful with the sick.

But she grew to fear Compline in the evenings, the stars of candlelight ablaze in their humble wattle church, when she knew she should think with love and prayer of all those she cared for, that God might guard them for the night. Through all the winter she had pattered her mindless prayers, but now suddenly there was nothing she could find to say. She tried to think of Dag, singing the same office in the great shadowy abbey at Dunfermline, and he was not there. She tried to think of Queen Margaret and the children in the rich warm castle on the rock at Edinburgh, and she groped at nothing in the shadows. She tried to lift her head and speak with God Himself, and the only prayer that she could find was the endless hopeless plea that He might let her die. Round her the thin singing of the nuns would change to the deep voices of men, strange and unearthly above wind whistling through the reeds, and the only name in her mind was Edward's.

It was with the coming of spring that her dead numbness began to wake to life. She thought she had known pain when Edward died and Gundred screamed at her that she had killed him, and she must know it true. She knew that now for nothing but a thin shadow of the agony that ripped her when the wind changed to the west and blew soft and sweet along the cliffs above a sea as blue as heaven; when the seagulls screamed and whirled over the grass with the sun white on their spread wings, and in the hollows of the cliffs primroses grew as they had grown last year, when all unthinking and unwilling she rode down to London. All around her, life was waking to a new year, and she must wake with it whether she would or not, and waking, know that Edward would not share it.

She knew now that it was true, as she had never known before. The year would rise, and again and yet again, to every year there would be another spring, but for Edward never. In the desperate knowledge, from which she had hidden all the winter, came some strange healing, with the mortal pain, and with it honesty that she had lost.

She walked into the hospice from the sweet cool wind along the cliffs, salt in the air and the tide tearing into the bay as though it would never make the shores. She looked round the half dark, airless place, packed with the poor and the ugly and the lame and the blind; with their stumps and their sores and their terrible patient faith. The whole crowded room stank of their sickness and misery, and the handful of sisters bustling among them could do no more than touch the edges of it. These were Queen Margaret's poor, to whom she had vowed to give her life, and having given it, to love them.

"Oh, merciful God," she whispered, and the spring wind teased at her veil through the open door. "Oh, merciful God,

I hate them. What am I to do! I hate them!"

Chapter Twelve

The wild spring winds which tore at Merca's bitter penance whistled down the glen at Dunfermline, and in the dark night Dag lifted his head to the desolate honking of the wild geese flying south, and knew the spring had come. Steadfastly he stared into the darkness and told himself that it would be the same as other springs; the blue washed skies and the fierce exciting thunder of water in the glen; the small flowers that he might copy in his letters; the pigeons cooing in the tower court and suddenly the sun, warm upon his head. Carefully he thought of all these things that God had given him before and would give him once again, and he numbered them on his fingers, and told himself determinedly that they were good.

When it was done, he stared into the dark, and knew that it was not enough.

"And what," he told himself fiercely, "if my sister be gone, and will not be back. I am grown now, and have no need of her. Almost I am old enough to be a monk."

With painful strength, each morning he faced his day in careful pleasure of all the things that he had loved, and did not know that those who loved him had all the winter watched his round blond face grow thin, his blue eyes shadowed with loneliness he would not admit.

The queen had looked at him with concern when she had ridden from Edinburgh in the middle of the winter, coming upon him in the cloister where she visited the monks.

"Dag!" she had cried before she could stop herself.

"Madam," Dag had said, standing from his colors to bow to her, and she bit back the words she would have said, for how could she say to him that he looked like the sad poor child who had first come to Dunfermline; his composed face as now, bitterly determined to trouble no one with his troubles. Nor could Dag say to her that to see her was like a candle in the dark; the nearest thing to seeing Merca; sister; Merca.

Firmly he closed his lips. He was come here to be a monk, and must learn to live alone. And she was a queen who must not interfere too much with the good master of the novices who had charge of all the boys. Well she knew why Dag grew thin and pale with his pathetic look of dignity, and it was not because his beloved monks were making him unhappy. She sighed, and laid a hand a moment on his cheek, and passed her way along the chilly cloister.

Carefully, one evening after Compline, when the sky above the hills was trailed with ragged clouds of wind and rain, he shielded a candle across the dark spaces of the courtyard. He was following Dom Benedict, on his evening round of all his sick. The wind tore at his candle flame and threw wild shadows on the tall black back of Father Benedict, and Dag sighed and wished it were not his task to go with him, and be his light. He hated the infirmary. Here all the sick of Dunfermline came for care and nursing they could get nowhere else, no more even here than a heap of straw and a thin woollen cover, and a hand to bless them and a voice to say a prayer if in the end they died.

The long dark room frightened Dag, full of smells and crowded with sick ugly people tossing and muttering on their beds of straw. The shadows of his candle flared across the ceiling, and eyes watched from all the shadows, filled with some terrible plea oppressing him with his helplessness that he could do no more than pad after Dom Benedict and hold his candle; and so often it seemed that the father himself could do little more.

Quietly Dom Benedict went down the long row, detaching grasping hands, and soothing desperate requests, a hand here and there on feverish head or wounded limb, a word to the two brothers who were on duty.

A figure on the straw held out a long skinny arm and croaked at him, and Dom Benedict bent down with sudden interest.

"Ah," he said, turning around to Dag, "he will do after all. Well he was young and strong." Dag knew he spoke only to himself, and gave no answer. One of the other brothers called him urgently from across the room, and his long eyebrows rose at Dag.

"Can you do more son, than hold a candle? Put it on that chest, and give that lad a drink of water."

"And don't you dare to tell me that you can't, and well I know you loathe it," said the firm humorous expression, and Dag looked at the monk a long moment and then laid the candle down. Carefully he took the dipper and sank it in the bowl of water, then knelt beside the straw.

It came as a surprise to him to find that the creature was a young man. His thick brows creased against some held belief that to be so sick you must be very old. He found he was pouring the water down the boy's neck, and with a small determined sigh, he placed a hand beneath his head and lifted it. Only then he saw the gaping wound across one side of it, which Dom Benedict had covered with some green pasty stuff that came off on his hand. Somehow in the flickering light he calmed his leaping stomach, and held the dipper steady while the boy took great thirsty gulps, one after another until the cup was empty.

Some strange pleasure filled Dag to see the look of ease on the boy's half-conscious face, and as he laid down his head, the vague eyes cleared and opened.

"Merca," said the boy, and Dag dropped the dipper in the straw.

"Who?" he said, glancing desperately around for Dom Benedict. "Who?"

The boy seemed to have trouble holding open his tired and sunken eyes, but "Merca," he whispered again, and fixed them on Dag, as though he begged him to keep him conscious until he had told him all he need. Dag was as urgent as he. Dom Benedict could come back at any moment, and he wanted no grownups in this as yet, if this was who he thought it was. Tall, Merca had said, and hard and slender. Tall, yes, thought Dag now, but no more than a bag of sorry bones. Fair, Merca had said. Such hair as was not covered in green paste was so matted with dirt and long-dried blood that it had no color of its own. But desperately he bent close.

"Who," he whispered, "are you? What is your name?"

The exhausted eyes fixed him for a moment so long and weary that he almost wept that they would drop before the boy could speak. Then at last.

"Edward," he said on a breath. "Edward." The eyes were closed and he was gone. The soft slither of Dom Benedict's feet came up behind Dag and he scrambled for the dipper in the straw, his mind whirling with excitement.

"Good," said the priest. "Good. We will make more than a candleholder of you yet."

"Good Father," said Dag. "Good Father, will he live?"

Dom Benedict looked faintly surprised, peering down his long black length at the small anxious boy.

"Oh, yes. Oh yes. He had a fever from his head wound. I have put a cleansing ointment on it, and his fever is gone. He will be well."

Dag breathed a long careful breath, and carried the candle for the rest of the round in a blind unseeing trance, with desperate care, lest he draw attention to himself. Never had it seemed to take so long, but in the end the moment came when he placed his smoking candle in the row along the cloister chest, and bowed to Dom Benedict as he passed into the monastery. Slowly Dag crept out, and sat down in the windy moonlight on the bottom of the cloister steps, his brain whirling, and his hands clasped firmly in his lap, as though by holding them together he might hold the plans and counter-plans that chased themselves across his mind.

On one thing he was certain. There must be no grown-ups. No matter what would happen after, there must be no grown-ups. They would want to do things by all the correct ways, indeed they would probably say that they could not be done at all. But he could not do it all alone.

That boy. That dark boy with curly hair, who had come with Merca and Edward's mother, who had made more noise about the court than they had heard since Madam the

Queen's sister had gone away. That dark boy, who it seemed was Edward's friend. Manfred!

Manfred had been kept by Madam the Queen at Dunfermline because he was a skilled silversmith, beating out and shaping exquisite vessels for the new abbey. Manfred! Dag looked up the hill to the light pouring from the tower at the high edge of the glen. They would be at the evening meal. The small black figure rose from the step and went firmly up the hill. By now he should be ready for his night prayers in his own sleeping room with all the other boys, but that was nothing to all that he meant to do yet, with God's help. They could put all his sins together and deal with them when he was finished.

Manfred came out of the evening hall among the last from his low place at the table, and as he left the lighted door a hand tweaked at his tunic from the shadows.

"Be off with you," said Manfred, seeing the small wide-eyed boy. "Be off with you!"

"Manfred!" Dag was almost in tears. If Manfred made a noise, he might attract attention. Fiercely he pulled again at his sleeve. Better say it all at once.

"Manfred, Edward is here!"

Manfred froze like a hind taken with an arrow, then wheeled into the shadows after Dag.

"What did you say?"

"I said Edward is here!"

"What do you know of Edward?"

"I am Merca's brother!"

"Dag!"

"Yes, yes, Dag. And Edward is here and, Manfred, we must get Merca."

Manfred took him by the arms and eased him further

away into the shadows.

"Now slowly, little Dag. Tell me what you know."

"I only know that Edward is in the infirmary." He told of how he had heard the boy crying for Merca, and in the moonlight he saw Manfred nod his head.

"It must be Edward. But how is he alive and here?" Then he said: "Why do you wait? Let us tell everyone, and get the news to his parents, and let me see him!"

Fiercely Dag grabbed him.

"No! No! First we must get Merca."

"But why! Surely Merca will be brought home as soon as she knows Edward is alive."

Frantically Dag strove for words. Like his other self, he knew his sister. If time were allowed to pass and she was given leave to think, then all sorts of foolishness like conscience would hold her back, and heaven knew what silliness she might decide on; like staying in that convent, even with Edward living. Desperate in his own loneliness, Dag told himself fiercely that it was all for Edward's sake and Merca's. Even Manfred, who had not known her long, had seen enough of her to know that what Dag said was true. She must not be allowed to think.

"How long to this nunnery?"

Dag thought. "A long night's ride.

"Have you a horse?"

"The king has."

"What do you mean?

"Having lived here so long," Dag said pompously, "I know the way of kings." Manfred snorted. "There are four horses always saddled, night and day," Dag went on, "lest there is some urgent message from the king that must not be delayed. There are always horses ready."

"You do know the way of kings." Manfred's voice held new respect. "But can we reach them?"

Dag looked at the sky. Nightly, from his small pallet bed in the boys' dormitory, he looked across at the unshuttered window, watching the progress of the idle moon, words forming in his head as the pictures formed beneath his brush. But this was not for Manfred. Only the terse statement: "Soon the moon will be gone. The sentries do not bother much. When it is cold, they go inside by the fire. The horses are tied along the rail behind the stables."

"But how do we get out?"

Dag frowned at so foolish a question.

"Why would they stop us going out?" he said. "They cannot see us, and if we are going out, then we are not an enemy. They will take no heed."

And in the small easy court of Dunfermline, that had not known a lifted sword for years, and in the absence of the king and queen, Dag proved entirely right. The four horses stood content and unattended along the hitching rail, the sound of cheerful voices coming from the firelit warmth within the stable quarters. The sentries at the bottom of the hill looked up only to call a blessing on their journey as they pounded off into the night.

"What if we were an enemy?" Manfred said aghast.

"The Queen and King of Scotia do not have enemies," Dag answered him breathlessly, and Manfred thought of how he and Edward had spent the last few years, and wished that life could be so simple.

Edward! It must be true he was alive, but how? He could think of nothing else.

He looked at the small black figure ahead of him in the darkness.

"You know the way to this place?" he shouted after him, and Dag looked back, clinging perilously to his horse.

"Well," he said. "We shall go along to the ferry and then follow the pilgrim's road. But," he added to Manfred who had drawn beside him, "I am but an indifferent horseman so do not, I beg you, ride too fast."

How we will laugh about this, thought Manfred, riding steadily through the starlight above the sea. How we will laugh, Edward and I! Of all the strange disordered things that we have done together, I rank it top to be riding here into the dawn behind this small determined cleric. He could, he thought, have found the way there by himself. Once they had reached the ferry where the boats plied over from below the great spur of Edinburgh, the night was alive with the creeping torches of the pilgrims, following the track beaten by the thousands of other feet before them, over the high moors to Kilrymont and the relics of Saint Andrew.

Dawn showed them all around on the road, in such great slow-moving numbers that Manfred could only thank God's mercy they had not ridden over any of them in the night. Dawn also showed the poor unhappy Dag, in his black cloak streaming in the wind, thumping along unevenly on the king's fastest horse, never so ill-ridden in its life.

"Dag," said Manfred anxiously. "What about the horses? What will happen to us about the horses?"

Dag was only half his age, yet his odd elderly composure drove Manfred to ask him as though he was the leader. "What will happen about the horses?"

"We have not stolen them," said Dag unevenly. "We will bring them back." Manfred crossed himself and rolled his dark eyes to heaven, and hoped that this would be enough.

"What if the king has an urgent message?" he asked then,

almost to see what Dag would say.

"The king is in Edinburgh," Dag said practically. "Anyway," he added in a moment, "Merca will make everything proper with the queen."

And Manfred smiled, hearing him in that small remark no more than the little boy he was. But he could not shelter behind any child, and he hoped when they returned to Dunfermline he could keep the skin on his back.

Dag fell silent, having little breath for anything more than holding his great horse and sticking to its back, even after Manfred stopped him once daylight had come, to shorten up his stirrups.

"It is not long now?" he asked of the tired face up against the misty sky, and Dag shook his head.

They did not have to search for Merca when they reached the convent, and Manfred breathed a prayer of thanks. He had found no answer to the problem of how they would find her if she was not easily to be seen. Dag in his black clothes was his only hope. They might allow him in. But as they cantered into the courtyard of the nunnery, Merca crossed it toward the hospice, lifting her astonished head from the cowl of her habit, to see the small ungainly figure of Dag, followed by Manfred, his grin as gay and cheerful as when he flirted with the girls at Westminster. They had laid no plans for their coming nor for what should be said, so both of them at once cried out to her.

"Merca! Edward is in Dunfermline!"

"Merca, Edward is alive!"

She hardly heard them—did not really understand them, except that their smiling faces and the mention of his name was all she needed. Alive! Edward! "And come!" they were saying. Urgently, leaning down from their horses, and poor

Dag like to topple on his nose. "Come," they were saying, "at once with us, to Edward!" Manfred reached his hand, and from the corner of her eye she saw Mother Gertrude, eyes and mouth wide open, advancing from the row of cells.

Dag was right. She did not stop to think, and had she thought, she would not have gone with them. But taken by surprise, there was no room for anything but honesty—breathless tears and wild delight—and seizing Manfred's hand and vaulting up behind him on his horse, her gray habit lifting to her coarse woolen stockings. Vaguely she saw Mother Gertrude and the clucking nuns who followed her, and the sick crowding to the hospice door at the scent of something strange. All vanished as Manfred kicked the great chestnut horse and turned him in a spatter of mud and stones and flying cackling geese, Dag whirling somewhere in the rear. They came into focus clearly only as the horses passed the monastery gates and she saw them all against the slate gray misty sea, small gesticulating figures already strange and from some distant past; crowded in a group of wattle buildings that she had never known.

They rode home slowly, resting the horses, and watering them at a small stream rushing down from the rain-drenched hills. They sang small foolish songs that she had refused to sing in London, and all the time the words and music only told her that Edward was alive; Edward; Edward. They pulled Dag down exhausted and beaming from his huge black horse, and Merca rode it, struggling with her long coarse skirts, Dag up behind her that he might have a rest.

"And tell me Dag," she would say every time he fell to silence. "Tell me every single thing that happened. What he said, and how he looked, oh tell me everything!"

Delighted, Dag would tell her, over and over again, every

smallest thing that he could find to tell, until he came to the part of telling how he looked. Then he halted lamely, for how could he say to her: "Sister, he is but a filthy bag of bones with lice crawling in his clothes and a gash in the side of his head that you could put your fingers in." Merca, seeing him tired, let him alone and remembered Edward for herself.

They dare not ask for food at the ferry hospice, with Merca in her nun's gown, and they avoided it, taking the inland paths, coming up the long slope to Dunfermline on the second evening, their horses gaunt and hungry as themselves; all of them silent now, knowing that however good all their intentions, they would have to reckon with all the people who had made the rules.

"The man in the stables is my friend," Dag said suddenly and firmly. "He will not mind about the horses."

They did not answer him. Merca was looking upward at the spread of wooden buildings that was the monastery, and trying to tell herself that in them Edward lay. Facing frantically the problem for the first time of how she could actually see him, since she, a woman, could not enter the infirmary.

No one took notice of them as they rode up through the wattle dwellings crowding at the bottom of the hill; nor past the monastery at which Merca looked with sick desperate longing; nor until they rode into the open court below the tower, when Queen Margaret's chamberlain moved out the door and came to meet them, followed by a groom.

Formally he bowed as they clattered to a doubtful stop, the horses sidling toward their familiar groom, who looked at them with horror on his face.

"Madam the Queen," the chamberlain said, "is waiting for you in her chamber. She bids you come immediately."

Three pairs of eyes stared down at him, and three mouths opened in dismay.

"Madam the Queen!" he answered as though one of them had said it out loud. "Madam the Queen," he said, "rode in from Edinburgh in the morning of yesterday."

Silently they clambered down and followed him into the dark bulk of the tower.

In all her years in Dunfermline, Merca had never seen the queen so stern. So very much a queen who must be bowed and curtsied to, and stood before in absolute humility, waiting for permission before they even spoke.

"Your vows broken, Merca," she said after a long cold silence. "Fleeing from the convent in a manner that will be the talk of Kilrymont for generations! Dag missing from the monastery so that these poor good men were mad with their anxiety for what had happened to him. Two of the king's best horses ridden into the ground. And all for what?"

Merca realized it was a question, but she was too astonished to give answer.

"But, but how did you know?" was all she could say. "Madam," she added belatedly.

"Messengers were sent at once to Edinburgh," the queen answered. "You did not hurry home."

Manfred made a wry grimace, and the queen put her hand up to her face.

"Madam, we couldn't," he said, "Dag—was tired."

Poor Dag looked tired. His round face was woebegone and filled with guilt, his black cloak spattered with mud from his long unhappy ride. Desperately he drew himself up and gave the queen his most formal bow.

"Madam," he said, "it was all my doing. They would have done nothing were it not for me. You see, Madam," he added earnestly, and took a step forward that he might come closer to make her understand. The queen's lip trembled and he sighed to see her so very angry. It made it more difficult. "You see, Madam, I thought my sister would not come, if she were allowed to think about it."

Deeply he breathed with relief, as though that were all the explanation needed, and looked surprised when Queen Margaret asked him: "But why did your sister need to come? She was in a convent."

"Edward, Madam," Dag said urgently, too tired to care whether he made sense, edging closer toward her knees in their crimson kirtle. "Edward. He is in the infirmary down the hill."

"Edward. Ah, Edward," said the queen. There was a long pause, and Merca did not dare to lift her head to see her anger. Then Queen Margaret said, "He is not down the hill." Sharply Merca looked up. The queen started at the expression on her face, and she began to smile.

"I have had him moved up here with the people of my own household who are sick. My own physician is caring for him." Merca had begun to shake from head to foot. "Gently, child, gently, he will be well."

Manfred was still puzzled, but aware that the air was clear and he might speak.

"Madam. They told you we had taken Merca from Kilrymont. But how did you know about Edward?"

"When I reached here, Dom Benedict told me of this youth who had crawled in here some two weeks back, and was now well enough for some reason to be most urgently seeking me. I bade him find his name, and when he told me, I did not find it hard to know why you and Dag had gone for Merca. But you, young man," she said then severely to Manfred, "what of your part in this?"

Dag drew himself up, and said firmly, "I took him with me."

"Ah?" said the queen, her fair eyebrows lifting to her hair.

"Madam." Manfred's open face was never more earnest. "Madam, it is true he took me, for I would not have known where to go alone. But Madam, it was not at sword's point." He tested the atmosphere, and dared to smile a little. "I knew him right about Merca. I knew that if she were given time to think, she would not come. And I knew that whatever had befallen Edward, he would need her."

His curiosity overcame the last of his fear. "Madam!" he cried abruptly. "What happened to him? We took him to be dead!"

Now Merca had begun to weep softly, sweet counterpart to all the hours she had lived with the certainty she had caused Edward's death. Clumsily Dag reached up and put a black-sleeved arm about her shoulders, and the queen shook her head.

"No one has asked him yet. He is not yet strong enough for talking overmuch. I thought," she added, gently, "that Merca should ask him now when she goes in to visit him."

The Queen smiled at the blind radiance breaking across the girl's face, still streaked with tears and dust.

"Now?" she stammered. "Now, Madam!" and the queen smiled and nodded, and was shot suddenly with a stab of lonely pain for being young, and knowing love at its first coming. Merca was already gone, pausing only for a hasty curtsy that was more a scramble through the door, her nun's kirtle gathered in her fists. Dag looked after her and yawned prodigiously.

"I knew" he said, "that she would want to come."

The queen laid an absent hand on his tired head, and nodded Manfred his dismissal, but her eyes were on the door curtain fallen behind Merca. Merca. Dirty and untidy, trailing a nun's habit on a horse across the moors of Scotia, with her eyes alight with love! Deeply the queen sighed. Now, Lord, she thought, dismisseth Thou Thy servant. All these long years that she had struggled to heal Merca's wounds of loneliness and terror, and in the end the healing had belonged in the stranger's hands of this boy who waited for her now.

For awhile when she came they could not even speak, his tears as weak and helpless as her own. He was in a small chamber by himself, propped with bright bolsters beneath a coverlet of crimson wool.

Feebly he plucked at it, and searched for words that would not be too much for both of them.

"She has been good to me," he said, "your queen."

Merca lifted her head and looked at him.

"And to me," she said gravely. "And to me." Then she fell again to staring at him as though she might never see him more, touching his pale cheeks and his hair and the edges of his sleeves with hesitant fingertips, trying to believe that he was real.

"Oh, Edward," she said in the end and knew it true. "Oh, Edward," and there seemed little more to say. Then urgently, despite the physician's instructions that he must not talk, she asked him, "But Edward— how? How?"

He had to search for breath to say enough, and his grin was as weary as his words.

"They didn't want us," he said, and she nodded, thrusting away the bitter recollections. "But they took me to be a soldier! Me, a Norman soldier! They were taking anyone.

Me!" If he had the strength he would have laughed, and she smiled delightedly to see the expression on his face. But he was exhausting himself, and he paused a long time before he tried again. "Ran away," he said. "From York. Robbed a hen roost to get some food. Some churl threw a club at me. But I found the way. I found the way."

"And nearly found me gone forever," she thought in anguish, and watched the tired lids drooping on his eyes. Suddenly they lifted.

"Never again," he said clearly. "Never again, my sweet!"

Wildly she grasped his hands. He could not leave her now. Frantic she kissed his cold pale face, and Edward close beside her cheek opened one impish eye. "Never again," he said once more.

"Never again, what, Edward!" She did not understand him, terrified that he might still be at the edge of death.

"To kill a king," he said. "To kill a king. We shall have better things to do." And was asleep.

"Edward," she said to his sleeping face. "Oh, Edward, Edward, I have a dress of ruby velvet you have never seen!"

Down the hill the small Dag knelt swaying with drowsiness before the novice master, and listened to his penance.

"Yes, my father," he said to each instruction, and the flame of the candle on the table hazed and blurred before his eyes.

"Yes, my father," and *"Mea culpa,"* and all the things that he should say, and his fair head was bent in true contrition. But his long mouth smiled and smiled and smiled, and could not stop.